Shadow Apprentice

The Garrison Creek Chronicles
Book 1

Linda Browne

Shadow Apprentice: The Garrison Creek Chronicles, Book 1

Copyright © 2024 by Linda Browne

Publisher: Crooked Mile Media

Cover Design: Jessica Bell

Disclaimer: This is a work of fiction. Any resemblance to actual persons, living or dead, events or locale is entirely coincidental.

ISBN 978-1-7390183-0-6 (eBook)

ISBN 978-1-7390183-1-3 (Paperback)

For Elka and for Kate

Chapter One

ection A: Spell Work (55%)

Question 1: A. If r = velocity and b = mass, calculate the sum of thrust. B. Which would be the better weave-in, Butler's variant or Simpson's? C. Explain. D. Calculate thrust, then weave in the variant, to produce a standard Start-and-Stop operational spell.

Ermin's eyes crossed. She read the question again, but it didn't make any more sense the second time around. She tried again. Words darted back and forth, like a school of tadpoles. Dread boiled in the pit of her stomach. What if she couldn't solve any of the other problems? It had happened before, the last two times she'd written the qualifying exam for the Guild's Apprenticeship Academy.

She imagined the look of resigned disappointment on Miss Fetchkeep's face. St. Anselm's Training School for Orphans had the highest placement rate of all the schools, but no student, anywhere, had ever failed the exam three times in a row. That sort of notoriety belonged to her, and it was now a part of St. Anselm's legacy.

She'd be fourteen next year, too old for an apprenticeship. If she didn't pass this exam, then where would she be?

On the shop floor of some factory, if she was lucky.

She clenched her fists. She could fix almost anything. She just couldn't calculate magic. Everyone knew that magic and machines didn't mix. She didn't see why she should be forced to learn something she'd never use. *Because the Guild says so, that's why.*

"All entrance candidates must possess a basic knowledge of spell casting before being admitted to the Academy." Ermin had combed through the Guild manual in search of exceptions so many times, she almost knew the entire thing off by heart.

All this worrying wasn't getting her any closer to finishing the exam, was it?

She took a deep breath to steady herself, then looked at the paper again. More questions flooded her mind, replacing the ones on the page. How could a letter equal a number? Were you only supposed to minus the parts inside the brackets? How could a bunch of equations add up to speed? If only they'd given her something to build, a mechanical problem to solve, not concepts that bore no relation to the real world! With proper tools, she could do something. With spells, there was nothing to touch, nowhere to hold on.

The grim atmosphere of study hall didn't help. Musty black curtains smothered every window. The air smelled of cracked pencils and chalk dust. At the front of the room, sand sifted through the inverted funnel of the hourglass timer with merciless precision. Study hall was the kind of room that sucked the juice out of every thought and made her feet itch.

She couldn't afford to waste any more time on useless ruminations. She'd come back to Spell Work later. She turned the page.

Section B: Mechanical Drawing (30%)

Ermin's breath came out in a relieved whoosh as she picked up her compass and triangle. A bewitcher (spell caster) was something she could understand! Mechanical drawing was also one of her favorite subjects. She was considered one of the best drafters in the school. Mr. Forge, the mechanics master, had said so. She wondered if the Guild examiners would give her extra credit if she pushed the question further. She hoped so. She'd planned for it.

On a separate sheet of paper, she drew another bewitcher, showing how possible modifications could be made to the original design. Why did the spells have to be written out on paper before being hand-cranked through the machine to activate them? They could be fired off so much faster with voice activation. She spent a long time with her design, wanting to make it just right. No one would ever guess that she'd already built a prototype for her best friend, Colin. She'd placed scrubbers alongside the microphones in his bewitcher, but the principles were the same. Once she was satisfied with her work, she moved on to Section C, History of the Guild (15%). Since she'd already taken the exam twice before, she flew through these answers.

If she'd cracked Sections B and C, then all she needed were six more marks.

Six more lousy marks stood between her and an admission to the apprenticeship school.

Since there was no telling if she'd be awarded extra credit for her designs, she'd have to find those marks somewhere in the blasted Spell Work section. Taking a deep breath, she went back to the beginning of the exam and skimmed through the questions. Colin had coached her on a couple of common spells and one of them appeared on the exam. She filled out the equations from memory, not understanding a single calculation she wrote down. Who cared, so long as she got it right!

She still needed three more marks.

A steady stream of whispers from a girl at a nearby desk shattered her concentration. One of those magi-tech brainiacs, no doubt. Ermin shot her a glare that soared right over the girl's head, which was bent down so low that the tip of her nose touched her exam paper. The sibilant whispers from the girl continued as her pencil flew over the paper, and her lips stretched into a pleased smile.

Ermin leaned across the aisle. "Would you please be quiet?"

"Silence!" Mr. Forge called out.

Blasted embers! That's all she needed, to be accused of cheating. The maniacal whisperer shot Ermin an unfriendly glare and cupped one hand over her paper as if to protect it. The whispers continued. Ermin longed to silence the whisperer with a swift blow, but she stilled her hands, fearful of being expelled from the exam hall. She was going to wipe that smug smile off the whisperer's face, though.

Infusing her voice with a menacing growl, she said: "Shut up, or I'll rip your yammer right out of your head as soon as we're done."

The whispers abruptly ceased.

Ermin sat back in her chair and continued flipping through the paper. Her satisfaction at silencing the whisperer quickly evaporated as she read through the questions again. Each one was more complicated than the last. None of them made any sense to her. They never did.

At the front of the room, Mr. Forge turned over a smaller

hourglass. "Last half hour," he called out. "Please make sure to review your answers."

Review? What a joke! How could she review what she hadn't even written down? Ermin cast a quick glance around the room. Everyone was still working. Where was she going to find three more marks? She flipped through the pages several more times. The Spell Work questions were self-contained and sequential: she couldn't pick them apart to find a mark here and there; she had to answer all the parts and come up with a calculation at the end. She couldn't do it. The realization oozed through her, like a sickening poison. Ermin clapped a hand over her mouth to stop the swear words from pouring out. All of that work for nothing.

"Is everything all right?"

Ermin looked up. Mr. Forge was standing next to her desk. The mechanics master was Ermin's favorite teacher. She couldn't answer.

"May I see?" Mr. Forge picked up the exam paper and flipped through it. "Your mechanical drawings are excellent— some of your best work. Are you sure that you don't want to try the spells?" He flashed her an encouraging smile.

Somehow, the smile made everything worse. Ermin stood up so quickly, her chair crashed to the floor. Her best work didn't matter. Being the best drafter in the school didn't matter. Not even being a good mechanic mattered. The only thing that mattered was learning how to calculate the spells the Guild Masters required of all apprentices. She couldn't do it. Her mind was a blank. Her entire life was a blank. She ran.

Ermin dodged and splashed through the streets of St. Andrew's market. Not even the rain was enough to wash away each awful thought. It was perverse, the way she could remember each question word for word, but when it came to the answers, her thoughts kinked up like bits of bent wire. Never mind the exam —she couldn't even make sense of herself.

Miss Fetchkeep must know by now that she'd failed. Ermin didn't know how she was going to face her. Maybe the head-mistress would kick her out of school. She surely would by Ermin's next birthday. Fourteen was too old for school. More than ever, Ermin needed to make her own way in the world, but it was illegal for the unapprenticed to make money at a trade. That hadn't stopped her from racing to her workshop straight after the exam to read the messages from her illegal clients. Essey Sykes, apprentice to Chen and Kim, millers, needed a storm wand fixed. So Ermin grabbed her tools and headed out to answer the call. Colin usually went with her, but he was busy taking a test of his own. She hoped it went better than hers.

Ermin shook herself. Self-pity was dangerous on the streets of Garrison Creek. Kids like her had to keep their wits about them. The storm would blow the street gangs right out of their hideouts, eager to snatch an unsuspecting kid. She stomped down hard in a puddle. Icy water soaked all the way through her boots to her wool stockings, which sagged and bunched in sodden lumps around her toes. *Good.* The discomfort of cold, wet feet was nothing compared to what could happen if she continued to mope. There was no telling who might be hiding in the old settlers' log shanties, or whose eyes might be watching her through the greased cloth windows.

She quickened her pace. She knew the back lanes so well, her feet took over, turning left, then right, then leading her up the tin roof of a shed and across the slate tiles of a shanty. Her boots skidded on the wet tiles, but she didn't fall. Instead, she crouched into the slide just like she was flying a carpet, using the momentum to nimbly hop across to the next roof. It was harder to hide up here on the rooftops but easier to see down into the streets below. She'd know soon enough if she was being followed.

If she wasn't so afraid of being snatched up by some gang and pressed into service, the view from up here might almost be pretty. It was as if a cloud had deflated over the streets to drape the stalls in an opaque gray curtain. Ruined buildings and ramshackle houses pressed close, like people huddled around a fire barrel on a cold winter's night. Ducks and chickens wandered through the rubbish-strewn yards. The rain dampened the usual stink of rotting garbage and cesspools. A red banner over a used-clothes stall stood out in sharp relief, like an apple dropped on a muddy street. Fog lamps bathed everything in a fuzzy yellow glow.

Wind gusted from the lake, strong enough to whip Ermin's black hair around like a Gorgon's striking snakes. She brushed it out of her face and adjusted her tool bag, an old apprentice's satchel she'd bargained for. Most gangs wouldn't risk pressing an already-claimed apprentice into their ranks, but Rory Smythe, King of the Wharf Rats, wasn't like most gang leaders—and her route threaded right through the heart of Wharf Rat territory. She cast a wary look back over her shoulder, but there were only empty rooftops behind her. Safe enough for now. She slid down the drainpipe into Trader's Row.

Carpet and horse traffic hadn't lessened one bit. Iron-rimmed wheels and hooves churned the streets into a brackish froth. One luckless boy had been caught on his carpet without a rain broom. He frantically swept at the growing puddles with his hands, but the rain and spatter from the passing traffic proved too much for the poor carpet. It sank into a muddy rut with the boy's boots still caught in the riding straps. He swore and bent to unbuckle himself, not noticing the transport wagon bearing down on him.

Without thinking, Ermin darted forward and yanked on the carpet's mooring rope, pulling it out of harm's way just as the wagon splashed past. The boy tumbled off, red-faced and breathless.

"You don't need a broom to get airborne," said Ermin. "This is reed cloth. All you need to do is shake it out. See? It'll shed water like a beaver." She snapped the carpet as if it were an old towel. Water arced through the air. The carpet rose.

The red-faced boy snatched the mooring rope from her hands, jumped onto the carpet, and sped off without a word of thanks.

"Some people have no manners," said a drawling voice behind her.

Denny Lorde, John Smith's apprentice, stood beneath an awning, his fluffy black hair framing his face like a puffball. His dark brown skin was smudged with soot from the smithy's fires. He pulled something out of his pocket. "Do you have time to settle up?"

Ermin looked into the dim confines of the stall. A shopkeeper's apprentice nodded to her in greeting. Ermin had fixed a broken heater for her last week. "Always," she told Denny. It would be safe enough to conduct business here.

She and Denny turned their backs on the street, pretending to be interested in a mound of muddy turnips. She was too wet for the awning to do her much good, but it kept her notebook dry when she pulled it from its oilskin wrapping. She flipped through the pages until she came to Denny Lorde's account. "Dragon Lord"—Denny's nickname—topped a row of lined and numbered columns. "What do you have for me?"

Denny opened his fingers. An entire packet of Speedwell's Acceleration Threads lay on his scarred and callused palm.

Ermin blinked. She couldn't believe what she was seeing. Speedwell's were seriously expensive, used to boost speed in the finest of carpets. "Where did you get these?" she asked in a low voice.

"Let's just say I collected on a debt of my own." Denny touched the side of his nose with one finger. "Is it enough to cancel my debt to you?"

Ermin seized the packet before Denny could change his mind. "It's enough." She recorded Dragon Lord's transaction and zeroed out his account. The threads were so costly that by all rights she should count herself as indebted to Denny, but she couldn't afford to gain a reputation for softness.

"Watch how you use them. People will take advantage if you're not careful."

"Repeat those same words to yourself the next time you look in a mirror, Denny Lorde. You didn't need to give me the whole packet."

"Each one for everyone. We orphans need to stick together. Does Miss Fetchkeep know you're keeping accounts?"

Ermin cringed inwardly. Denny had inadvertently exposed her greatest fear: that Miss Fetchkeep, who'd set Ermin up with a workshop, would discover that she was illegally trading her jobs for credit. This went against Guild rules, and the Guild was St. Anselm's biggest patron.

"I'm only collecting trades and favors."

"I doubt that makes much difference to the Guild. It's only a matter of time before Miss Fetchkeep finds out."

"Are you suggesting that I work for free?"

Denny flashed her a lopsided grin. "Not me! I'm only warning you to watch out for blackmailers."

Ermin laughed. "I'd like to see the apprentice who'd dare try to blackmail me! Their masters would throw them out on the streets if they discovered that somebody else was fixing all their gear." Though it was beyond her how any master could expect an apprentice to have any mechanical knowledge when they spent all their time learning spells.

"It's not us apprentices I'm worried about. It's the other students. How many of them know that you're trading?"

Denny had a good point. Ermin's trading was more or less an open secret among her apprentice clients, but what if someone from the school found out and told Miss Fetchkeep? She'd have to choose: boot Ermin out of the school or risk losing the Guild's favor. No guesses as to which choice she'd make.

"If they know about your workshop, it's only a matter of time before they find out the rest. All I'm saying is, watch yourself."

With that, Denny Lorde slipped out of the stall and was gone. The sharp corners of the Speedwell's packet dug into Ermin's palm as she stowed her prize in the bib pocket of her coveralls. She was taking no chances with it slipping out. She'd always been terrified of being caught and kicked out onto the street, but now she had something tangible to show for all the sleepless nights.

She tucked her notebook with its oilskin wrapping away too. The loss of it would be just as disastrous as the loss of the Speedwell's. If Miss Fetchkeep kicked her out, she'd now have something to sell and a book of favors she could collect on. No way she was giving those up, not even for Miss Fetchkeep.

She was about to step onto the street when a scrawny hand reached out and pulled her back inside the stall. It was the shopkeeper's apprentice, her lips thinned to a tense line. And no wonder.

The Magistrates were driving their latest captures to Redemption Square.

People pushed up against the sides of the stall to clear the road. The patter of rain on the awning didn't mask the groan of wooden wheels as a tumbrel trundled into view, drawn by eight haggard people. Despite the cold and wet, they were clothed in little more than rags. Most went barefoot. A dozen or more terrified figures huddled together in the open bed of the wagon. Everyone knew that those prisoners had committed no crime except to be born with the so-called heretical powers of wizardry that Garrison Creek's Chief Magistrate, Dr. Dean, was determined to stamp out. Ermin anxiously scanned the faces of the prisoners inside, but Colin was not among them. Neither was their friend Georgie.

A grim squadron of guards escorted the tumbrel, their black capes flung open, exposing bewitchers strapped to their chests. *Magistrates.* Ermin would recognize them anywhere. Anybody would. The bewitchers hummed as the Magistrates swiveled their wrist nozzles to and fro, ready to fire stunning spells into the crowd at the slightest provocation. People on either side of the road bowed their heads, either in fear or to avoid looking at the prisoners. Nearly everyone knew someone who'd been carted off to Redemption Square. Ermin's fists clenched in fury, but she cast her eyes down like the others.

"Queen Georgina must have been mad to appoint Dr. Dean and his goons to rule over us." The shopkeeper's apprentice's lips barely moved as she spoke. "They're not fit to govern a chicken coop."

Such talk bordered on the treasonous, even if most people hated Dr. Dean. Ermin tried to make a joke. "Maybe the Queen was desperate to get rid of them."

"Then she should have thrown them into the ocean. Now I suppose we'll have to do it ourselves."

Ermin squeezed the girl's arm in warning. "The tumbrels will come for you next if anyone catches you talking like that."

The shopkeeper's apprentice gave her nose a fierce wipe with one sleeve. "Easy for you to say. You don't live by

Redemption Square. You can ignore the drainings. You don't see them being carted off afterwards like a load of dead animals. It's a wonder that anyone survives in the Scrawlings at all."

The Scrawlings referred to a ring of scrubland between Garrison Creek and the forest, where wizards were exiled once they'd been drained of their powers. The lucky ones were claimed by bandits—if *lucky* was a word that could even be used. Ermin had had her own experiences with gangs. The memory was a dark one. She pushed it down.

A throng of people followed the tumbrel and its grim cargo, eager to witness the spectacle in Redemption Square. Some even carried food baskets on their arms, as if they were going on a picnic. Others held skipping children by the hand.

"You'd best slip out the back way," said the shopkeeper's apprentice. "Watch yourself."

"And you."

After the tumbrel departed, regular activity returned to the streets. Ermin hefted her tool bag and joined the throng headed toward Picking Cork Lane, a mud-soaked trail that led to the mill. Ermin had rejigged the millers' storm wand two weeks ago. It wasn't a good sign that it had broken down again so soon. She didn't relish telling Essey that the conductor plate was likely fried, but that was the least of her problems. Working at Chen and Kim's would take every bit of stealth and wit she possessed, if she wanted to keep her business safe... and secret.

Chapter Two

The rush of water from the Don River grew louder and louder as Ermin walked down Picking Cork Lane. The stone foundation of the Chen and Kim Milling Company rose from the water, its high wall sheltering the wooden gears and huge grindstones inside. Outside, the water-wheel creaked and groaned. The wall climbed up another two stories to an attic topped by a sharply peaked roof. A hook and pulley system swung out over the side yard, where Hetty Chen was loading grain into a basket. Her partner, Soon-Yi Kim, was busy hauling the grain up to the attic, where it would be cleaned before being funneled through a series of bins and chutes and ground down into flour. Bits of chaff drifted free from the birdlike beaks of Hetty's and Soon-Yi's masks, worn to keep the most recent outbreak of tree fever at bay. Ermin was glad she was immune to the fever and didn't have to wear such a mask. Woven from thick cloth, they looked heavy and hot.

The mill's living quarters jutted into the street like an afterthought, and were surrounded by a porch roofed with moss-covered tiles. Two stone steps led down to the road. Standing on the bottom step was Sclaw, the Faeling cook.

Faelings, or human–Fae biracials, weren't common outside of Pennyluck Place, the settlement's roughest neighborhood. But Sclaw was not only the mill's guardian and protector, she was Soon-Yi's adopted sister. Nobody messed with her, at least not if they wanted to do business at the mill. Sclaw's great wings were folded neatly on her back, and she was clothed in her best tunic and talon guards. A basket hung from her arm. She was about to either run a few errands or take her half day. Either way, it would be safe for Ermin to work. Essey was just as keen as any apprentice to keep her mechanical illiteracy a secret from her employers, so she always summoned Ermin during those times when Sclaw would be out.

"Remember to take the buns out of the icebox," Sclaw said, while Essey listened with crossed arms and an impassive expression. "They'll take at least two hours to rise. Don't forget to set the hourglass." Sclaw unfurled her wings and wrapped them around Essey. "I won't be gone long."

"Sclaw!" Essey cried out in muffled protest.

"Oh, you youngsters!" Sclaw's wings retracted and gave Essey's shoulder an affectionate squeeze. "Always so embarrassed about everything!" She adjusted a large white mask over her nose and mouth. Faelings weren't immune to tree fever either. Sclaw's leather talon guards scraped down the stairs and left a trail of three-toed prints behind in the mud. "I won't be long, my dumpling."

Ermin ducked back into Picking Cork Lane as Sclaw lumbered past, still rumbling instructions over her shoulder. When she could no longer hear the thump and scrape of claws, Ermin stepped out of the alley and waved to get Essey's attention. Essey spotted her and signaled her over. Ermin raced to the porch.

Essey pulled her inside. "Hurry—Sclaw's got periscope vision. She can see around corners."

"I hope she can't see through walls."

"I'm not sure, but her mother can."

Ermin laid down her satchel and opened the storm wand's control panel.

Essey watched with interest. "Isn't Colin with you?"

"Not since Mr. D'Arcy shoved a fancy new bewitcher into his hands and invited him to join the elite class." Ermin fought to keep her voice light while a wave of jealousy surged over her. If she had half his abilities, she could have passed her exams long ago.

"Fancy that old demon D'Arcy doing something so nice! When I think of how much I hated him when I was at St. Anselm's... Never mind. I'll keep watch in case Sclaw comes back. You can hide under that table if she does." Essey indicated a side table, whose folded wooden leaves reached down to the floor. "I've polished it with lemon oil so she won't be able to smell you."

"Well, that's a comfort." Ermin crouched down before the storm wand. It was just as she'd suspected—a blown-out conductor plate. "You'll have to order a new one," she said, tapping the blackened plate.

"Can't you fix it?"

"No, I've rejigged the generating coil too many times. The plate's burned clean through."

"Isn't there some other way to restore the electricity? They're bound to ask me to come up with a solution as soon as you're gone. What will I say?"

Ermin sat back on her heels. She couldn't manufacture a conductor out of nothing. She listened to the rhythmic rattle and creak of the wooden gears downstairs. It was almost hypnotic. Bits of chaff sifted through the gaps in the floorboards. Soon-Yi's and Hetty's voices rose and fell, like the clacking of gears. The millers were taking advantage of the strong currents in the water to grind as much grain as they could before the river froze over and the axles stilled into the long silence of winter.

The axles—of course!

"Essey, where's your bicycle?"

"It's just outside. Why do you ask?"

"I think we can restore your electricity by pedal power. At least until the conductor plate comes."

"Brilliant!" Essey's face broke into a grin. "I knew you'd think of something!" She raced outside and returned wheeling her bicycle.

Ermin removed the back wheel and stripped off its cog, bolting it to the storm wand's driveshaft. "There! Now all we have to do is attach the chain and find a way to prop up the rest of the frame."

"I see! Pedaling the bicycle will generate power for the storm wand in the same way that water powers the crankshaft downstairs."

"Exactly. Maybe I should hire you as my apprentice."

"Not a chance. I'm going to set up my own bakery one day." Essey dragged a couple of crates across the floor. "Here, we can use these ironwood crates to prop up the frame. You know, I quite fancy the idea of riding my bicycle in the kitchen. You should set yourself up in business once you leave school."

"First, I have to qualify for an apprenticeship." A bare-thin chance she had of it too, when she couldn't even remember the calculations for the most basic spells. "I'm no good at magi-tech, though. I can't calculate a spell to save my life."

"What do you need magi-tech for?" Essey kicked the crates into place under the bicycle. "Machines don't take to spells. How many times have you told me that?"

Ermin pressed her lips together. Shame and frustration spread through her like a stain. No other student at St. Anselm's Training School for Orphans had failed the Guild's exams as many times as she had. Although she counted the apprentice miller among her friends, Ermin couldn't bring herself to tell Essey what had happened.

A two-noted whistle pierced the air, mimicking the call of a marsh cray bird. Ermin would have recognized that signal anywhere. She and Colin had used it countless times. "It's a warning from Colin."

Essey flew to the window. "The Widow Pettigrew's just landed. And she's brought Pickle too. Quick, under the table!"

There was no time for Ermin to gather up her tools before three loud knocks sounded on the front door. She scooted under the table. The Widow Pettigrew's elderly pug dog, Pickle, was nothing if not inquisitive. Maybe the lemon polish would throw him off the scent.

A cool breeze blew into the room as Essey opened the door. "Good afternoon, Mrs. Pettigrew."

"Ah, Essey. How are you faring, my dear?" Iron-rimmed wheels creaked as the Widow Pettigrew drove her wicker wheelchair into the room.

Although the hanging wooden leaf obscured Ermin's view, she knew exactly what the Widow looked like. Her usual top hat would be perched on her head, secured under her chin with a flowered scarf. She'd doubtless be clad in a scarred pair of leather flying jodhpurs and rubber flying goggles. She'd designed and built the flying wheelchair herself, which she wheeled and flew everywhere, her muscular brown arms navigating air currents and road ruts alike with ease.

"Are Soon-Yi and Hetty in?" the Widow asked. "Since the post is so unreliable, I decided to deliver my monthly donation to the Orphan Fund myself. All right, Pickle. Down you get."

Seconds later a beige pug appeared under the table, his hindquarters supported by a wheeled metal platform. At the sight of Ermin, he erupted into a chorus of excited wheezes. Before he could bark out a welcome, Ermin seized him in her arms, wheeled platform and all. Pickle snorted and licked her face, wagging his tail so hard it was difficult to keep the platform from bouncing around.

"Soon-Yi, Hetty!" Essey shouted. "The Widow Pettigrew is here!" She lowered her voice. "What do you think of our new invention over here by the stove?"

Wicker strands popped and creaked as the Widow Pettigrew shifted in her chair. "Is that a bicycle-powered storm wand? Most ingenious!"

Boots pounded down the stairs, silver buckles clanking. "Emma!" Soon-Yi's voice rang out. "What a pleasant surprise!"

"I do hope I'm not interrupting you," said the Widow Pettigrew.

"Not at all. We're just sitting down for a tea break. Would you care to join us?"

"If it's not too much trouble. It's very daring of you to get your own. I'm surprised that Sclaw even allows you in the kitchen."

"She's gone for her half day. She may chase us out when she returns."

The pump started with a rusty shriek. Water spewed into a tin kettle. Ermin scratched Pickle under his chin. The pug's eyes closed and his head grew heavy. With a thump, he collapsed onto her lap.

"Before I forget, here's my next month's donation for the Orphan Fund. I wanted to bring it myself, as the post has been rather unsatisfactory of late."

A second pair of boots clomped across the floor. "Indeed, it has," replied the husky voice of Hetty Chen. "It was most kind of you to deliver it yourself."

"That way I know the right people are getting it. By the way, I need to pick up a few bags of flour."

Ermin stifled a yawn. Sclaw she'd been prepared for—not the mind-numbing boredom of a tea party.

"How many?"

"A baker's dozen, my cook says." A baker's dozen was thirteen bags, and the Widow Pettigrew lived by herself. Ermin wondered why she'd need so much.

"You're in luck. We've just sacked a fresh batch."

A flare of lemon-yellow fire lit the edges of the table, followed by a muffled boom. Pickle jolted in Ermin's lap and barked. She was forced to release him.

"Oh no!" the Widow Pettigrew gasped. "The drainings have started."

"Poor souls," Hetty murmured.

Ermin imagined Colin and Georgie chained to the draining platform in Redemption Square, too weak to duck at the rotten vegetables and fish guts thrown at them by the large, jeering crowd.

"I don't know how people can bear to watch such a spectacle." The Widow Pettigrew's voice shook with anger.

"We've never gone," said Soon-Yi, "and we never shall."

"It doesn't matter if the drainings themselves don't kill anyone," the Widow Pettigrew said. "Banishment to the Scrawlings in that condition amounts to little more than a death sentence. Those so-called Magistrates are no better than murderers."

Ermin clapped both hands across her mouth to smother her own gasp. The Widow Pettigrew's declaration could be construed as treason. The Magistrates had imprisoned people for far less. That the three women had spoken so openly was a sign of deep trust not only in each other but also in Essey. For the first time since arriving at the mill, Ermin's shoulders loosened. The world outside might not be any safer, but a welcome of sorts had been kindled inside this kitchen. She couldn't wait to tell Colin and Georgie that the mill's inhabitants, along with the Widow Pettigrew, were wizard sympathizers.

"I do hope that dear Sclaw won't be harassed," continued the Widow Pettigrew. "You know how rough the crowds can be."

"Sclaw had an errand to run before visiting her mother, who lives well away from Redemption Square," Soon-Yi said. "She'll steer clear of the crowds."

"Well, that's a comfort. Gracious, look at the time! I must be off. Pickle, come!"

A chorus of excited snorts and scrabbling claws greeted this announcement.

"Look at him go!" Soon-Yi marveled. "He's gotten quite skilled at using his chair."

"Indeed, he has. I'm lucky he's still alive. I've got Norris D'Arcy to thank for that. Do you know him?"

"I wish I didn't."

"His looks are fearsome, I grant you, but he's really the gentlest of souls. Nearly a year ago, Pickle disappeared. I looked everywhere but he was nowhere to be found. Three days later, D'Arcy appeared at the door holding the poor mite. He'd suffered a massive stroke, but D'Arcy quite restored him."

Ermin thought it far more likely that D'Arcy himself had caused the stroke. The gaunt, black-cloaked magi-tech teacher terrified everybody at St. Anselm's. His piercing dark eyes had a way of picking you apart, as if he was deciding what use he might make of you, or possibly one or two of your vital organs.

"All except for his back legs," the Widow Pettigrew continued. "I don't know what kind of spell D'Arcy used, but I'd swear that Pickle has more energy today than he did before his stroke." Her iron-rimmed wheels scraped across the floor. A gust of wind blew in, colder now. "Thank you for the tea, my dears. Until next month."

"We'll see you out." Soon-Yi and Hetty accompanied the Widow Pettigrew onto the porch.

Essey's face peeked under the table. "Hurry!"

There wasn't any time for Ermin to grab her tools. She followed Essey up the stairs to the attic, where she climbed into the hauling basket.

"I'll bring your tools to the workshop later," Essey promised.

Ermin gave her the thumbs-up as Essey let her down into the side yard using the pulleys. Denny was right. Nearly every apprentice in the Creek owed Ermin favors. All it would take was one pair of loose lips blabbing to the wrong person and Ermin would find herself being blackmailed or kicked out of school. Maybe both.

She ran around to the back of the house. She'd have to take the towpath. Swollen with late autumn rains, the river tumbled by in white-green whorls and eddies and foamed over the path. Ermin's boots got wet again, but soon the land rose to a hillock. Ermin pursed her lips and whistled. Her marsh cray call wasn't as convincing as Colin's, but it was good enough to unearth a familiar blond head from a pile of bracken. Ermin wasn't surprised that Colin had chosen that particular spot with its clear view of both the street and the river. She'd expect nothing less from a good watcher, and Colin was the best. Ermin slowed her stride. Running up a hill at full tilt would only look odd, and here in the Creek the merest hint of oddness could make people turn on you as quickly as the weather.

What had made Colin skip school this time?

Chapter Three

"You missed one of your messages," Colin said, handing it to Ermin as they walked away from the mill. "It's from Georgie. The ink's still fresh. That's why I came. And before you ask, nobody saw me."

Ermin frowned down at the paper bird in her hand. Its wet wings quivered one last time. A chill shivered through Ermin's body. No matter how often she told herself that the message birds were nothing more than folded sheets of spell paper, the stillness—when it came—felt like a death.

She unfolded the paper bird to read the message inside. The purple scrawl did indeed belong to Georgie Scratch, their close friend and a former St. Anselm's inmate.

Sunday, November 15, 1829, at your earliest convenience.
BonMot

Sunday, November 15, was today's date and the note was signed with Georgie's nickname.

Ermin crumpled up the message bird in her fist. "That

pincer press they use is finicky at the best of times, but Georgie usually gives me more notice than this."

"Her conjurements are usually better too."

"Keep your voice down!"

"Nobody's paying us any mind. They're all too busy watching the drainings, aren't they?" A note of bitterness crept into Colin's voice.

"Let's hurry," said Ermin, worry starting to grow in her mind.

A young person in a rush was a common enough sight in Garrison Creek. Miss Fetchkeep often sent orphans out on errands. The trick was to appear as if they weren't together so they wouldn't stick out, so Ermin and Colin headed to opposite sides of the street. Apprentices always included a precise time in their messages to tell Ermin when their mentors were away. It troubled Ermin that Georgie had specified no time. There was no telling whether or not the printer Rustman would be there at the shop when they arrived. Worse, the print shop was still blocks away. Georgie must have been in a hurry when she wrote the note—not a good sign. Hurry meant danger when you were an orphan in the Creek.

"We've still got a long way to go," Colin said, echoing her thoughts. "Maybe I could—"

"No! We can't take any chances, not so close to Redemption Square." Ermin pointed at a rusty expanse of pipe attached to a tiled gutter three stories up. "Rooftops—it's the quickest way."

She shimmied up the rain-slick pipe with practiced ease and Colin followed. Freezing water flowed over Ermin's hands as she grabbed hold of the gutter and hauled herself onto the roof. It was a good thing she and Colin were so small. Otherwise, the drainpipe might have collapsed under their weight.

The leaden belly of the sky pressed down on them. Smoke

rose from the chimneys, sinking like fog in the humid air. Ermin didn't see them, not at first. They rose in a ragged huddle from behind one of the smokestacks: kid snatchers, wearing yellow-and-black-checked scarves. Ermin fairly threw herself off the edge of the roof and scrambled down the drainpipe, pushing Colin down.

"Wharf Rats!"

They slid to the ground as five greasy heads peered over the edge of the roof. One of them pursed her lips and blew out a three-noted trill. A similar cry echoed from several blocks away.

A signal.

Ermin raced back down Picking Cork Lane and into a maze of back alleys. She needn't worry about Colin; if they got separated, he knew the back ways as well as she did. Windows flashed past, like pictures in a gallery. In one sat a tailor, costly yellow satin spread out across his lap. Another revealed two gamblers tossing wooden dice across a gaming table. Another showed a large family sitting around a table in a very small room. Thick tallow candles illuminated the watery bowls of soup laid out before them. Still, the family clasped hands with such joy that Ermin had to look away. Memories rose up to tug at her like a moat full of hungry carp. She pushed them away.

Rare beams of sunlight broke through the clouds and bathed the buildings in a warm golden glow. It would have been beautiful if Ermin and Colin hadn't also been simultaneously lit up, so that they were little more than moving targets. They ran past yards where rows of moon cabbages grew at the bases of ancient dung heaps. Sweet smoke from resinous rock ember combined with the reek of rotting vegetables from numerous cellars. Loud shouts erupted from the doors of a tavern as patrons staggered out, some with their arms draped around brightly dressed street walkers. No matter how far

Ermin and Colin ran or which way they turned, the trilling cries pursued them.

Sweaty and out of breath, they stopped to rest against one of the original log cabins built by the settlement's first immigrants. Ermin was a fair runner, but even she couldn't keep up the pace. "They're tracking us from the rooftops."

Not only that, but their escape had led them to the refuse fields behind St. Andrew's market, where grocers dumped the old or spoiled leavings from their shops. They'd come to the very heart of Wharf Rat territory, where Rory Smythe, their rat-faced leader, ruled with an iron-tipped cudgel. "They're herding us."

"Are they?" The tips of Colin's fingers flared red.

He didn't even need to chant the conjurement out loud. He disappeared, winking out of existence as if he'd never been. It was a disorienting experience for Ermin to look down and find herself invisible, with no physical limbs to anchor her in space. It was hard to tell whether she was standing or floating. How could she move without any legs? Not until hoarse whispers crept down the walls, and several pairs of Rat boots thudded down, did Ermin discover that her invisible legs worked just fine. She slipped past the four Rats who'd fanned out to search the street. She passed right under the dark silhouette of a fifth Rat who watched from the roof. Not one of them noticed her.

It wasn't until she reached the end of the alley that she even dared to whisper. "Colin?"

A spoiled squash rolled across the road, bowled by an invisible hand. It hit the signpost for Ink Street and burst open, its bright orange guts splattering everywhere. Ermin felt her invisible lips curve into a smile. Rustman's shop was located in Ink Street. She set off at a run toward whatever trouble lay ahead.

～

Ink Street was a riot of paper. Discarded flyers swirled through the air. They stuck to Ermin's legs as she and Colin morphed from smoky outlines in just a few steps. Colin must have used a timed conjurement. Only when Ermin stood beneath a wooden sign engraved with the rust-colored image of a pincer printing press did she bend down to peel the wet sheets away, relieved at the sight of her own hands. She didn't know what she'd do if she ever lost them.

Ermin flung the flyer away in disgust. Who were they kidding? Only those who could pay the hefty entrance fee to the ball were welcome, and you had to be able to afford all those fancy clothes besides.

Colin appeared at her side, his hands brushing away the clinging sheets. "Do we go in?"

Despite the rain and cold, the door to Rustman's Print Shop stood open. The wrongness of it shivered across Ermin's skin like a frosty gust. "We'd best take a look around outside first."

She strolled past the shop's windows. Each mullioned pane had been rubbed with thick streaks of soap to obscure the interior of the shop from curious passersby, especially any stray news hawkers looking to make a quick penny. Old Rustman didn't want anyone stealing his stories before he had a chance to release them. Cobwebs had hardened in the corners of the windows like blackened strands of spun sugar. Ermin circled back, checking for any Magistrates who might be patrolling the area. That she didn't see any didn't mean that Georgie was in the clear. Her boot slipped on a card lying underfoot: a black card with a white lightning bolt. She jumped back as if the bolt had struck her.

Colin was by her side in an instant. He let out a gasp of recognition. "Wizards' Resistance!"

Ermin gripped his arm in warning. Saying such a thing out loud was enough to get you carted off in a tumbrel. As for anyone found in possession of a card like that... well, it didn't bear thinking about.

"There's more than one."

Colin was right. Cards bearing lightning bolts fanned out on the road right in front of Rustman's. A horrible suspicion wormed its way through Ermin. "You don't think... "

"I'm going in."

"No, wait!"

Colin dodged around her, using a conjurement to evade her grasp. His body melted into the brick wall. Ermin's temper nearly boiled over in a familiar mixture of terror and anger. It was nerve-racking being dragged into Colin's madcap schemes without warning.

The interior of the shop was almost as cluttered as the streets. The pincer press squatted like a six-legged insect in the center of the shop, its seven pincers dangling. A large collection of type cabinets ringed the press. Each cabinet contained a series of very thin drawers divided into small square compartments made to hold small metal letters and numbers. The drawers, called cases, had been pulled clean out and the metal letters and numbers were strewn everywhere except for a cleared path around the table—the kind of path an apprentice's feet might make if she were circling the table to get away from an angry printer.

Colin re-materialized beside her, his golden hair plastered with sweat and his rosebud cheeks shining. "She's not here. I've checked all the rooms."

He pulled an apple from his pocket and took a big bite. For anyone else this might be a strange thing to do, but wizards were always in need of fuel, especially after they'd cast. The depletion or "blowback" from the conjurements he'd cast must be bad. At least he'd remembered to bring food this time. Ermin couldn't help feeling annoyed. Why had he bothered to waste more energy when he could just as easily have walked through the door?

"Where could she have gone?" asked Ermin. "She wouldn't just disappear, not after she sent for us."

"Not unless she had to."

A horrible feeling of foreboding took hold of Ermin. She inched closer to the table and swept aside the cases. Sheets of uncut card stock lay beneath. Each sheet showed rows and columns of white lightning bolts against a solid black backdrop.

"Blasted embers!" Colin breathed over her shoulder. "She really is working for the Resistance."

Ermin turned to face him. "Colin, this is really bad." Only then did she become aware of a lurid magenta glow blinking on and off again behind the door. She ran over and slammed it shut. A contraption like a spiked eyeball spun on a dusty length of silk ribbon. It was a wizard lamp, charmed to detect the presence of a wizard's conjurements, and either Colin or Georgie had set it off. Now its bloody spotlight shone down on both of them.

Colin jumped back in alarm. "Didn't know that old Rustman had one of those! Did I set it off?"

"Does it matter? We should have been somewhere else ten minutes ago. Don't run!" Ermin called after Colin as he bolted through the door. "It'll only draw attention."

Colin's response was to grab her hand and pull her into the street. "No time to worry about that! The Magistrates could be flying this way as we speak. Hurry!"

Colin led her behind a horse trough that obscured a narrow slice of space between two buildings. They only knew it was there because they'd sought shelter inside it one cold winter's night. It was a tight squeeze, much too small for any grown person to fit through. Even if the Magistrates arrived at the shop this very minute, they'd be forced to take the long way around to get to the other end. She and Colin would be long gone by then.

The narrow slip took them to Douglas Street, where a swift-running stream divided the road down the middle. A group of toshers squatted on the far bank. They swirled their hooked staves through the water, hoping to snag any valuable debris that had come downstream from the wealthy houses to the west. Of course, a stream had other uses as well.

Colin grabbed her hand and pulled her down the bank. "Come on," he said. "You know what we have to do."

Unfortunately, she did.

The toshers watched them curiously as they approached the steam. Colin went first.

He dove headfirst into the freezing water.

"Bit late in the year for a swim, isn't it?" one of the toshers called out as he surfaced.

Whoops of laughter greeted this witty remark.

Ignoring them, Ermin took a deep breath and jumped. The water was icy cold, but she forced herself to stay under until she was sure the magical residue left behind by Colin's conjurements had washed off. She surfaced with a gasp. At least the Magistrates wouldn't be able to track them now.

Colin was already clambering up the bank.

The toshers hooted louder than ever, slapping their knees in mirth. They sounded like a murder of crows at harvest time. Four shadows glided over the street. The noise abruptly died away as four figures in black cloaks swooped into view, conical black masks jutting out from their faces like beaks. *Magistrates.*

Ermin and Colin raced for the alleyway. Their wet clothes were a dead giveaway. One of the Magistrates threw an oblong pellet down into the street. It exploded on impact. They reached the alleyway just as green tendrils of tracking fog writhed forth, nosing the air like hungry snakes. Within seconds, all of Douglas Street was obscured from view. Ermin could hear the toshers coughing and swearing.

"We're trapped!" Colin said. "They'll search the alley for sure."

"Then we'd best take to the rooftops."

Ermin braced one foot against the outer wall of one of the buildings and, placing her hands on the adjacent building's wall to steady herself, pushed up to lift herself off the ground. She repeated the motion on the other side, bracing her other foot on the opposite wall to push herself still higher. Colin followed suit, bracing and pushing himself up the walls as the tracking fog billowed into the alley. When they reached the top of the buildings, they pulled themselves onto the right-side rooftop and lay down flat. Rough gravel scraped against Ermin's face. She hardly dared to breathe.

After what seemed like an eternity, she peeked over the edge of the roof. The writhing fog had melted away, having found no quarry. Her shoulders sagged in relief. The stream had done its job. The Magistrates flew off without a backward glance. A lone man driving a threadbare carpet brought up the rear. His stockings were mismatched and wrinkled, and his apron was stained with ink. A plain muslin cone-like mask protruded from the lower half of his face. Even so, Ermin recognized the fringe of grayish-red hair that bounced off his shoulders.

"Rustman." Colin's voice thickened with disgust. "I hope Georgie's gone far away from here."

A chill passed over Ermin. How far away could a runaway apprentice go before she was pressed into a gang, or worse? She and Colin had to find her, but how would they know where to look? If only she could sit by the water for a while and let her thoughts unspool, letting the snarls loosen until she could see her way clear. This was no time for dallying. When the Magistrates found the empty shop, they'd head out, looking for people to question. She and Colin didn't want to be here when they came back. She'd have to sort through the tangled mess later.

"Come on," she said. "We'd best get back to the school."

Where had Georgie gone? Ermin puzzled over it during their long walk back. No matter how hard she tried, she couldn't find an answer.

Chapter Four

Ermin and Colin entered the school grounds from the rear, bending double from the waist to hide their heads beneath the screen of the long grasses. The square brick mansion that was the school was barely visible. A glass cupola rose into the sky like a milky eyeball. It made Ermin feel as if they were being watched. They cut across the field to the Old Chapel, a stone building half-buried in vines and shrubs. It had once been used as a hospital for tree fever victims in the early days of the settlement. Maybe *chapel* was an Old World term for hospital. Maybe not, though, as nearly everyone had died.

Inside, vaulted walls rose to meet wooden beams that had once been covered with roof tiles and now lay bare to the weather. Vines crept along the stone floor and scrambled up the pillars. Ermin had to walk carefully to avoid tripping. At the end of a long aisle hung a moldering tapestry that concealed a flight of stone steps. Ermin pulled off her glasses and rubbed them free of finger smudges and rain spots.

"I'm boiling!" Colin declared as he unbuttoned his coat.

The fancy new bewitcher from D'Arcy was strapped to his chest. Its firing hose was made out of flexible plates of metal that followed every movement of his arm. A brass wrist guard and nozzle gleamed from under his shirtsleeve.

She pointed. "What happened to the one I made for you?"

"I left it in the workshop before D'Arcy summoned me to his office."

"What for? I thought you were writing some sort of test in his class."

"I was, but he said he wanted to test my spell casting." Colin waved his brass wrist nozzle with an elegant flourish. "Don't worry, I made sure I used this new bewitcher for all the spells."

That D'Arcy had targeted Colin for special attention and had given him a new bewitcher besides unsettled Ermin. "Miss Fetchkeep would pitch a fit if she knew he'd taken you out of class."

"Your lack of application is disappointing and self-limiting." Colin mimicked the headmistress's low-pitched croak. Even hearing Colin's imitation of the headmistress made Ermin feel oddly diminished. "Don't worry—she knew. She was already there in his office, waiting for us."

That tidbit of information only heightened Ermin's sense of unease. She pushed aside the tapestry. "Come on. I've got to kit myself out with some new tools. You need to ditch that new bewitcher for the one I made for you."

"But—"

"We don't know anything about it—how it works or what it really does."

"We know it's waterproof," said Colin.

"Maybe so, but it's safer for you to use the other one."

Colin's face hardened into stubborn lines.

"At least until I've had a chance look at the new one,"

Ermin hastily amended. "I've never heard of D'Arcy giving anything to anybody before."

Colin grunted. It was as much of an assent as she was going to get, and for that she was grateful. It wasn't easy to shift a wizard once they dug in their heels.

Because he could see in the dark like a cat, Colin led the way down the steps. Ermin followed. A solid bank of darkness rose to envelop her. She wished that she had a portable glim box to light her way, but she'd have to trust Colin's wizard-sight. It didn't fail her. They made it to the bottom without mishap.

Ermin's workshop was located inside an old burial chamber —a nice, quiet place if you didn't mind the stone coffins stacked up against the walls. With their lids ajar and the occasional shroud or bone peeking out, it was easy to imagine that the skeletons inside popped out now and then for a walk. They didn't scare Ermin. She'd seen enough tree fever victims lying motionless in ditches or carts to know that death was a commonplace in the Creek. The dead couldn't hurt you. It was the living you had to watch out for.

Her groping fingers found the glim box she'd mounted on the wall. She flicked it on. A warm light shone down over all her tools: cutters and drivers by the door; hammers, fasteners, and measuring sticks pegged to a board above the table. She'd scavenged each and every one. A grinning skeleton stood by the door.

"Hello, Horatio." Colin laid a friendly hand on the skeleton's bony shoulder.

Horatio had been the one lone skeleton that had indeed escaped his coffin. After fixing him with wire, Ermin had rearranged him into a standing position by the door as a kind of friend and guard skeleton. He'd been there ever since.

The bewitcher she'd made for Colin sat atop the workbench. Colin shrugged out of the fancy bewitcher that D'Arcy had given him and strapped it on. The small, square box with its crank and nozzle looked exactly like the machines everyone else used to cast spells, except this one required no spell paper and the crank was just for show. Instead, Colin wore a special glove that channeled his conjurements through scrubbers to remove any telltale colored residue left behind by wizardry, cleaning it to a smoky silver to make it look like he'd just finished calculating a magi-tech spell.

"I like the feel of yours better," said Colin. "The one that D'Arcy gave me is so stiff, it's hard to use. Bet you'll never guess what I found in his office."

"A dead body."

Ermin grabbed an old tool belt from under the table. It was small enough to hide under her St. Anselm's smock and contained a surprising amount of storage. She began to assemble a new tool kit, packing up her second-best lock picks, twisters, pincers, cutters, assorted hardware, and her prize possession: a raveling tool she'd fished out of the Douglas Street stream during the spring floods.

"Nice one!" Colin chuckled. "No, a flying carpet."

"Of course he'd have a flying carpet, Colin. How else would he drive to school?" Ermin unearthed a couple of spare glim boxes. "Heads up!" She tossed one of the glim boxes to Colin.

He deftly caught it. "I'm not talking about D'Arcy's flying carpet. I'm talking about a broken one that someone stashed behind his filing cabinet."

Ermin straightened. "Are you telling me that D'Arcy's got a broken flying carpet in his office?"

"That's exactly what I'm saying."

If it was broken, the chances were good that it had never been requisitioned. If it had never been requisitioned, no one would know that it existed, except possibly D'Arcy. He could hardly report it missing if he'd never reported its existence in the first place. Ermin considered this while she mended a tear in her smock with an old pin fastener she'd salvaged from a broken wrist guard. She was glad she'd saved it. You never knew when a particular thing might come in handy.

"You know what we're going to have to do, then?" Ermin asked.

"Oh, I do."

Ermin teased a loose brick from the wall, uncovering a square, empty space. She took the accounts book out of her pocket, wedged it inside, and replaced the brick. The book would be a lot safer hidden here. There was a soft scrape, as if a stone lid on one of the coffins had been pushed aside. "Colin, stop it! This is no time for fooling around."

"It's not me," said Colin.

"No, it's me," said a familiar voice.

"Georgie!" Colin shouted.

Ermin whirled as a tall, lanky girl climbed out of a coffin. Her dark brown skin shone with sweat. Her dark, curly hair was hidden beneath a tweed cap. She wore woolen trousers held up with a bit of frayed rope, and too-big boots that clopped down on the floor. The old pieces of newssheet she'd used to make them fit poked through the many holes.

"Georgie!" Ermin exclaimed. "What on earth are you doing here?"

"It was the safest place I could think of." Georgie pulled a battered leather saddlebag from the coffin and threw it down to the floor. "Listen, you two. I've gotten myself into a real pickle."

"We know," said Colin. "We've been to your shop."

"I couldn't wait, not after... Please, you've got to help me. I don't know where else to go." Georgie hefted her saddlebag, as if she expected to be driven away.

Ermin remembered that bag, the way it had thudded against Georgie's skinny back when Rustman had led her from the orphanage, crumpling Georgie's papers up in his fist without even once looking at her. The sight of that had made Ermin feel sick. The sick feeling was even worse now.

"Did Rustman catch you printing those cards?"

"He never should have! He was supposed to be attending a meeting of the Guild, only he forgot his specs. Forgot them all over again in the excitement of calling me a terrorist and a traitor. I'm surprised you didn't pass him in the street."

"How could you have been so careless?" Ermin snapped. Relief at finding Georgie was swiftly giving way to anger. "You've got a bounty on your head, thanks to that little stunt you pulled!"

"Do you think I don't know that?" Georgie's dark brown eyes, usually full of warmth and laughter, snapped like two ignited coals. "And don't bother telling me how stupid I've been. I know that too."

"If you knew it, then why did you print those cards?"

"Because I wanted to do something! You don't know how hard it is sitting around marking time, trying to pretend you're someone else, until you're found out."

"But joining the Wizards' Resistance—"

"They're the only ones fighting for us! Nobody else dares to stand up to Dr. Dean or his goons. I had to do something! So I put out the word. In the classifieds, in case you're wondering."

"Ermin, are you down there?" a man's voice called out. Footsteps clattered down the stone steps.

"It's Mr. Forge," said Ermin. "Hide!"

Georgie jumped back in the coffin. Ermin closed the lid but kept it cracked open so that Georgie could breathe. Colin kicked the saddlebag under the workbench, then slid in after it as Mr. Forge bounded into the workshop.

"Ah, there you are! I was hoping to find you here."

A trim, dapper man in his early twenties, the mechanics instructor exuded a playful energy that made him seem almost childlike. At least until anger struck. Then he was like a roused bull mastiff.

"I wanted to talk to you about this." He held out the exam. "No, don't pull faces! Your mechanical drawings were quite excellent, but this idea for a modified bewitcher triggered by speech instead of spell paper is exceptional. Did you know there are people working on that very thing? I wonder if Miss Fetchkeep would allow me to take you to meet them?"

"I doubt it." Ermin could almost hear the headmistress's voice: "Field trips are not for remedial students." Ermin was nothing if not a remedial student. "What's the point, anyway? I'll never pass the exams."

Mr. Forge fiddled with his white cloth mask. "Perhaps if you had special classes... "

"What's all this talk about special classes?" Miss Fetchkeep, the headmistress, asked as she entered the workshop. Her soft-soled slippers made no noise as she glided across the floor. She wore her gray hair up in a bun, her black eyes needle sharp behind her spectacles. She was wearing a fur-lined flying cape. It retracted its wings and folded itself around her shoulders with a purr.

"Oh, good afternoon, Miss Fetchkeep," said Mr. Forge. "I was just commenting on Ermin's excellent drawings and a most intriguing idea she sketched out. With your permission, I'd like to take her to the Guild Academy. It would be good for her to meet the engineering students, and I know they'd like to meet her."

"I think that Ermin has quite enough work to do at the moment. She has yet to pass her exams. Colin, are you in here?

It's no good hiding from Mr. D'Arcy. He expects to see you in his office before dinner."

Colin emerged from under the table, looking sheepish.

"Is that the new bewitcher Mr. D'Arcy gave you?" Miss Fetchkeep demanded. "What's it doing on the floor? Pick it up at once."

"Sorry, Miss Fetchkeep." Colin picked up D'Arcy's bewitcher, but he didn't take off the one Ermin had made for him. He left the room still wearing it.

"There's no doubt that Ermin has a fine champion in you, Mr. Forge," said Miss Fetchkeep. "Perhaps one day she may visit the college, as you say, but not at the moment. She's not ready."

Mr. Forge narrowed his eyes and thrust out his chin. The bull mastiff was emerging. "She's more than ready, Miss Fetchkeep. Her ideas are quite sophisticated. The exams are causing her too much trouble. Has she been assessed for learning differences? Perhaps if she received special tutoring... "

Miss Fetchkeep's black eyes snapped. "Our current magitechnician is a most able instructor."

"D'Arcy's only interested in teaching the school's magical prodigies. He neglects the rest of the class. There is no reason why Ermin can't learn how to calculate the required spells, if she gets some proper help."

"I will be the judge of what my students need and how well my teachers are performing, Mr. Forge. Kindly return to your class and leave the running of the school up to me."

Mr. Forge's face turned purple, but it was clear he'd been dismissed. He turned on his heel and left the workshop, taking the steps two at a time. They heard him push the tapestry aside so hard, it fell to the floor with a muffled thump.

Miss Fetchkeep patted Ermin on the shoulder. Ermin shivered. Although the headmistress wore gloves, her hands were always icy cold. "Don't fret over the test, my dear. You may lack the necessary magical aptitude for an apprenticeship, but you'll always have a home here. Would I have set you up with this workshop if I didn't believe in you?"

Ermin tried to smile, but guilt poked and prodded at her. If her account-keeping ever came to light, her deception would be unmasked and Miss Fetchkeep would know exactly how far Ermin had betrayed her trust... and so would the Guild. But she couldn't stop charging for her services. If she worked for free, the apprentices would lose all respect for her. Her "soft" reputation would follow her around like a stinking carcass, making it impossible for her to do business. What if Miss Fetchkeep found out about the trading and kicked her out? She'd have to make her own way in the world. She had to charge for her work. Only every time she did, her risk of discovery increased.

"I almost forgot. I have a gift for you."

Ermin watched in amazement as Miss Fetchkeep rummaged around in her reticule and pulled out a silver necklace. Miss Fetchkeep had never given Ermin a gift before, let alone one so expensive.

"I know that you don't care much for jewelry now, but that may change in a year or two. Here, let me fasten this around your neck." Miss Fetchkeep's fingers grazed the nape of Ermin's neck. Ermin suppressed a shudder. "There!"

Ermin looked down at herself. At the end of the chain swung a teardrop-shaped pendant of milky glass. A prism of light swirled on its surface. She wondered how much money the necklace would fetch. She guiltily squashed the thought.

"Doesn't that look pretty?"

Pretty was not a word Ermin associated with herself, not with her spidery limbs, pimply, dark olive complexion, snaky tangle of black hair, or the thick spectacles magnifying her already large yellow eyes. Fierce, resourceful, mechanical, yes. But pretty? It was a miracle that Georgie wasn't laughing herself silly inside that coffin.

Ermin fingered the necklace. It felt odd, not like something she would wear. "It's too good to wear to dinner," she told Miss Fetchkeep. "I'd better leave it here."

"Of course, my dear."

Ermin took off the necklace. She longed to stash it behind the loose brick where she kept her accounts book, but she couldn't very well do that with Miss Fetchkeep watching. Instead, she hung it on a hook and draped a rag over it.

Miss Fetchkeep wrapped an arm around her shoulders. Cold radiated through the layers of blouse and cardigan. It was like being hugged by an iceberg.

"Shall we go to dinner?"

Miss Fetchkeep made it sound like dinner was some fancy banquet instead of the usual potato, onion, and cabbage soup. It should have given Ermin a warm feeling to know Miss Fetch-keep was so fond of her. She should have felt grateful for the necklace. Instead, she felt almost ill as she accompanied the headmistress back to the school for dinner. She couldn't stop thinking about Georgie trapped inside that coffin, with the Magistrates combing the streets for her outside.

Ermin poked at the strands of boiled cabbage swimming in her soup. They looked like large sea worms. Dessert—stewed, reconstituted prunes—offered little respite. She tried to choke down a few more mouthfuls.

Colin slid into the seat beside her, which she'd kept vacant. His eyes were wild and he was out of breath. His cheeks were flushed—dangerously so.

"What's wrong?" she whispered.

"Not now. He's watching."

Ermin tilted her head down so that a screen of hair covered her eyes. Then she looked at the teachers' table. All of them were eating, except Mr. D'Arcy. The magi-technician was staring straight at them. He'd grown thin to the point of gauntness. His combed-over hair no longer hid his bald, slightly pointed head. His teeth, gray and mossy, poked between his lips like crooked tombstones. He inspected Colin with a kind of greedy appraisal. Ermin had once accompanied Miss Fetchkeep to the winter market to buy geese. Miss Fetchkeep had moved among the cages, poking and prodding with a knowing finger. Mr. D'Arcy might almost be a cook, sizing up a Colin-shaped goose.

"What's he got on you?" Ermin whispered to Colin.

"Wish I knew. He kept staring at me all the time I was in his office."

The answer was perfectly obvious, even if neither of them could admit it. D'Arcy knew that Colin was a wizard. Why else would he have singled Colin out for special testing?

Ermin would have left immediately after supper but for study hall. Mr. Forge usually supervised, but this evening it was D'Arcy who strode between the tables once the dishes were cleared away. He watched the students so closely that it took Ermin ten minutes to risk pushing a note she'd written over to Colin. Many long minutes later, the note came back, shoved beneath the edge of her primer. Ermin concealed the note inside a book and flipped the pages back and forth, as if she was checking some interesting fact, while she read the note's contents.

Passed exams with such high marks, D.'s taking
me out of class tomorrow for more "special studies."

She could almost feel Colin's panic through the paper. Her own heart thumped so loudly she was sure it had burst free of her chest. She glanced down fearfully, expecting to be confronted with a bloody mess, only to find the note dry and clean with its terrible message etched out in plain black ink.

Nothing had changed, except that everything had.

The school was no longer safe for Colin. Georgie couldn't hide out in the workshop very much longer, and Ermin's own days at the school were numbered. They had to run away. The only question was how. The answer flew into her mind almost instantly. Ermin scribbled out a hasty response and passed the book over to Colin.

We take the carpet—tonight.

Chapter Five

"You're deluded," Georgie whispered as they crouched together in the upper hall of the school.

Now that they were outside the door to Mr. D'Arcy's office, Ermin wondered if Georgie was right. If so, she wasn't the only one. "Oh, really? Then what do you call doing a print run for the Resistance right under Rustman's nose? Face it, Georgie. We left sanity behind a long time ago."

Georgie glared at her.

Colin laid a steadying hand on Georgie's shoulder. "We need this carpet. You know we do. Come on."

Silently, Georgie got to her feet.

Ermin eyed Colin with incredulity. How did he always know exactly what to say? It couldn't be some built-in wizard's talent, because Georgie had none of it.

The stone balustrades cast barred shadows over them as they shuffled along the upper gallery. The soles of their boots were muffled by towels they'd stolen from the laundry. Ermin hoped they wouldn't slip and fall on the polished marble floor. The carved stone peacock guarded the top of the newel post like a reproachful sentinel. Ermin half expected it to open its beak to shriek at them.

"I'd forgotten how spooky this place is at night," said Georgie. "Like a monster's castle. I always wondered how Miss Fetchkeep could afford it."

"Denny Lorde told me that this house once belonged to a wealthy merchant, whose family was struck down by the fever," said Ermin.

Georgie and Colin exchanged smirks.

"What?"

"Nothing," said Colin. "I guess that explains it. Nobody wanted to live in a plague house."

"Yet they thought it was the perfect place for us orphans," said Georgie. She looked nervously over her shoulder. "What about the night patrols?"

"I checked the schedule," said Ermin. "They won't come this way for a while. It's the perfect time to break in."

She pulled out her lock picks, but Colin and Georgie had already aimed their sparking fingers at the doorknob. It opened with an audible click. Colin slipped inside with Georgie right behind him. Ermin's exasperation threatened to boil over. She could have picked the lock in no time. There was no need for conjurements and the trail of residue they left behind. If the two of them would only slow down and think for once! She let herself into the office and locked the door behind her for good measure.

Heavy window shade panels had been unfolded and pressed flat against the glass. A good thing, since Colin was already shining a glim box around the room. Just as they couldn't see the outside, nobody would be able to see in. The glim box's roving beam picked out a heavy oak desk and chair at the center of the room, as well as several bookcases ranged along the walls.

"Hey, look at these fancy togs!"

Colin shone the light at Georgie, who was standing by a wooden mannequin. A fine suit made of jet-black velvet with a frilled shirt hung from the mannequin's still form. A sewing bot stood at the ready, its dial set to *alter*, its needles poised for action. Georgie took a high-brimmed top hat off the mannequin's head and slapped it on top of her own ragged cap.

"I've come up in the world since I left St. Anselm's."

Colin laughed, but Ermin was having none of it. "Quit clowning around! Where is this carpet, anyway?"

"Over by the desk," said Colin.

The desk was covered with an assortment of dolls, no doubt from the domestic arts classroom. Ermin tensed. The near perfect row of dolls mocked her. Domestic arts was the one subject she did more poorly in than magical technology. Her only consolation was that Colin did just as poorly in domestic arts as she did. Georgie had been expelled from the class after she'd charmed one of the sewing bots to sew Mr. Taylor's pants to his chair. Colin crossed the room to where a handsome black-and-tan flying carpet sat humming on the floor.

"We can't steal that!" Ermin protested in an alarmed whisper.

"Not that one." Colin was busy rummaging around behind a wooden filing cabinet in the corner. "There's another one over here but it's stuck. Help me!"

"We'd better hurry," said Ermin. "If D'Arcy's carpet's still here, that means he hasn't left and gone home, wherever that is."

"He's got swank digs in New Town," said Georgie. "One of those new builds they put up by the Fortress. I've seen him coming and going when I've been out on delivery." Georgie grunted. "This filing cabinet is heavy!"

"We've got to put our backs into it," said Colin. "On the count of three… "

Together, they pushed the filing cabinet out from the wall. It caught on the floor and nearly tipped over. A metal drawer popped open with a squeaking bang that reverberated around inside the cabinet. It took all three of them to right it. The drawers slid noisily back. *School Records*, an old, faded label on the front read.

"Pretty funny kind of label, when there's nothing inside," said Georgie.

"They're probably down below." Ermin pulled open another drawer. A smell of rust rose up to meet her. There was nothing inside that drawer either. The bottom drawer contained a rolling pencil and an old mug. There were no files, papers, or records of any kind inside.

Colin's head appeared around the metal frame. "Ermin? The carpet's behind the filing cabinet, not inside it."

They gave another mighty heave, exposing a dusty heap of rubbish. Ermin couldn't see anything that remotely resembled a flying carpet. "What am I supposed to be looking at?"

Colin placed Ermin's hand on top of the mound of debris. She gasped as her fingers snagged on some loose woolen strands. The dust heap gave a feeble flap.

"How did you find it?" Ermin asked.

"It kind of flapped at me, just like it's doing now. Only it didn't look like a rubbish heap then. I charmed it just in case D'Arcy happened to look behind the cabinet."

"He could have thrown it into the dustbin by mistake," Ermin said as they wrangled the dust heap to the middle of the room. As soon as they unrolled it, the charm faded away.

"I doubt if he remembered it was there. There was quite a lot of dust heaped on top of it already." Colin shone a beam over the carpet's gold, green, and red phoenix design. Although threadbare and faded, it was still magnificent. "More to the point, can you get it to fly?"

"Now?"

"Well, it's either that or carry it through the school to your workshop, which is the first place anyone will look for us. You can fix it. I know you can."

"I don't even know what's wrong with it yet." Ermin opened her tool belt, her fingers clumsy with nervousness. She ran her hands over the carpet, expecting to feel a familiar electric pulse. There was only silence. A faint buzz flared beneath her fingers for an instant before sputtering away. "There's a disconnection for sure."

"How can you tell?" Colin asked.

"It keeps stopping and starting. Here." Ermin grabbed his hand and held it over the sputtering spot.

"I don't feel anything."

Georgie laid her hand on the carpet. "Me neither."

How was that possible? That flutter was too loud to be missed.

"Can you fix it?" asked Georgie.

"I don't know."

Ermin's eyes took in the carpet, looking for the one thing that didn't fit. All flying carpets had control cords woven into them along with acceleration threads to calibrate the speed. As far as Ermin could tell, there was nothing wrong with the number of cords or threads; they just weren't connecting with each other. She bent down for a closer look. "Colin, can you shine the glim box on this worn patch over here?"

Colin obliged. Ermin could see the problem clearly: a frayed section near the steering column, where the interlocked pattern of cords and threads had been worn away. The integrity of the carpet had been breached. If she wove the hanging ends back into the existing pattern, the carpet might work. She pulled out her raveling tool. That's when she heard voices on the other side of the door, then the jangle of keys.

Georgie's hand clamped down on hers. "No time!"

Colin snapped off the glim box and kicked the carpet under the desk. He must have cast a conjurement because Ermin's entire body flattened out. She gasped, but her voice was instantly smothered, as if her mouth had been stuffed with wool batting. She could no longer feel her tongue. She could no longer hear her heart.

Light filled the room. "Ah, good. I'm glad to see that you've agreed to mark this week's sewing assignments," Miss Fetchkeep said in a low croak. "Mr. Taylor has just been released from the hospital. I'm sure it won't be long before he returns."

"I am happy to be of assistance," D'Arcy replied in his deep, gravelly rasp, though the stiffness of his tone betrayed his distaste for the task.

"Some of these dolls are quite cunning. They may be good enough to sell at the winter market, don't you think?"

"Mr. Taylor will be a far better judge of that than I."

The edge of the wooden desk dug into Ermin's back. All of her fingers on both hands were stuck together as if enclosed in tight mittens. She tried to move her head, but her neck was frozen into place. Her eyes remained fixed on the ceiling. Her vision was veiled, as if she was seeing through a woven linen mesh. She couldn't roll her eyeballs or blink. She couldn't even tell whether or not Colin and Georgie were beside her.

She caught a disconcerting glimpse of a pair of abnormally large spectacles hovering close to her. Two black eyes peered at her intently. Ermin discovered she couldn't shiver. Either she had shrunk, or Miss Fetchkeep had turned into a giant. A huge hand closed around her middle, lifting her into the air. Her stiff body pivoted to and fro and her limp arms swung as Miss Fetchkeep examined her. "This one is so lifelike. Look, she's even wearing a St. Anselm's uniform. This other one is a bold fellow, isn't he?"

A second giant hand seized the prone body of a rag doll. Ermin took in its cocky, white linen face framed with blond hair. Its blue button eyes stared unblinkingly back at her.

D'Arcy poked at the blond-haired doll with one crooked finger. "This one is vaguely familiar." D'Arcy's face was blown up to several times its normal size. His glittering black eyes and crooked teeth were nearly as large as Ermin's hand.

"Hmm." Miss Fetchkeep prodded a doll wearing a news hawker's cap and large, holey boots. "Are the orphans also repairing carpets?"

"What?" D'Arcy looked down. His frown deepened as he kicked at something on the floor. Ermin would have held her breath if she'd had any breath to hold.

"It's a most useful endeavor, considering the new tariffs. Poor Matron has actually resorted to running her errands on a flying doormat. Shall we attend to business?"

"Oh... yes." D'Arcy appeared flustered as he opened a drawer and riffled through some papers. "The preliminary report... "

"Why don't we retire to my sitting room?" Miss Fetchkeep said. "I have a fine bottle of brandy waiting—just the thing to keep out the chill."

Mr. D'Arcy's desktop loomed alarmingly into view as Miss Fetchkeep placed Ermin's face down on it. She couldn't see anything, but she heard the door hinges squeaking open and closed, a key in the lock, and the retreating click of boots in the marble corridor outside. She gasped as her body re-inflated. She nearly fell off the desk, but pushed herself upright with her newly reformed hands. The blond doll had disappeared. Colin sat up in its place.

"Dolls, Colin?"

"Sorry. It was the first thing that came to mind."

"Ugh!" Georgie sat up, rubbing her head. "I'll have nightmares for weeks. Do you think they recognized us?"

Ermin was certain that Miss Fetchkeep had from the way she'd drawn D'Arcy away, almost as if she'd been worried about the dolls eavesdropping. They jumped off the desk and onto the carpet. Colin snapped on the glim box for Ermin while Georgie stationed herself at the door.

"They might come back," she said.

Ermin didn't have any speed wool for the repair. The closest thing she had was the packet of Speedwell's Acceleration Threads Denny Lorde had given her. She slid out several of the precious threads and laid them flat against the carpet over the frayed spot. As she touched down the raveling tool, she heard the sound of something heavy being dragged across the floor. She looked up to see Georgie wedging the back of a chair underneath the doorknob.

"What? If they come back, this will buy us more time. Are you sure you don't want me to cast a conjurement over that carpet? It would be faster."

"A conjurement will ruin a machine quicker than water. I'll have to do this the old-fashioned way—by hand."

Ermin bent over the frayed patch. Raveling was tricky work at the best of times. Here, the speed wool was worn right through. The loose ends were too short to patch over the hole. She was going to have to use extra Speedwell's. She tilted the hook, slowly feeding in lengths of Speedwell's and weaving them around the frayed strands of wool to extend them. She wove the newly blended thread around the control cords that regulated speed and acceleration.

"Someone's coming," said Georgie.

Panic made Ermin fumble. The raveler fell from her fingers. Colin snapped off the glim box, plunging them into total darkness. The doorknob rattled as a key worked the lock. Ermin's fingers closed around the raveler. She straightened, her heart thumping in fear. The carpet rose a few inches off the desk, humming—airborne, at last.

"Get on, everyone!"

A silvery-pink conjurement came out of Colin's bewitcher and writhed and glowed in his hand. Clearly, Ermin hadn't entirely perfected the scrubbing function in her prototype.

"No!" She pulled his arm down, making a mental note to correct this. "You can't reveal yourself."

"I'm using the bewitcher," said Colin.

"Yes, but you're holding the conjurement in your hand. It's a dead giveaway. No magic like that ever came from just a bewitcher." Ermin unlatched the window and gave it a shove. The window shade panel fell off, but the window was stuck. She lay down on the carpet and kicked at the frame with her feet. Colin and Georgie joined her, banging and hammering, not caring who heard them. The window creaked open a few inches.

From behind came the sound of splintering wood as the door broke. The chair shot across the room and hit the desk. A cloaked and hooded figure stood on the threshold. Ermin kicked at the glass pane. No good. It was bullseye glass, thick as a bottle. With a hollow metal clank, the figure sprang. Colin let fly his conjurement. The window exploded outward in a red-tinged blast, leaving a few jagged pieces stuck to the rim like teeth.

"Hold on!" Ermin slapped one hand down on the activator button.

The carpet reared up and shot from the room.

Chapter Six

Ermin hung on while the carpet bucked and circled, climbing to tree height then dropping to brush the spiked tops of the surrounding fence. The first jolt of speed was terrifying: like being on the back of a runaway horse with only a mane to grip or, in this case, a fringe. She flattened her body, slipping and sliding on the carpet until she finally found the toe straps. She shoved her feet into them and grabbed at her glasses, which were hanging off one ear. Behind her, Georgie and Colin struggled to strap in their own feet.

With shaking fingers, Ermin straightened her glasses and rose unsteadily into a rider's crouch. She'd only been on a carpet once before—as a passenger. She had no idea of how to drive. The carpet flew into the trees. Bare branches stretched out skeletal fingers to pluck her off. She ducked and swerved. So did the carpet. Ermin ducked to avoid a large branch aimed at her head, then resumed her crouch. The carpet dropped, then leveled off. Legs shaking, she lost her balance and fell forward. The carpet sped up, heading straight for an ancient willow with a trunk at least three feet wide. Colin and Georgie both screamed. Ermin leaned backward and threw her arms around her head, bracing for impact. The carpet screeched to a halt. Ermin's forearms slowly came to rest against the willow's trunk, the rough bark scraping her skin. Slowly, she lowered her arms. Seismic ripples ran through the woolen pile at her feet, but the carpet stayed put in a restless hover.

"It's acting like it's bewitched," said Colin. "All that speeding about. What did you do to it?"

"Me? You know I'm no good at spells." A switch clicked on in Ermin's brain. "I must have raveled in too many acceleration threads. No wonder it's so fast."

"We might be glad of that...eventually." Colin looked nervously back over his shoulder. "Maybe we should get going."

St. Anselm's rose up behind them like a one-eyed ogre. Wet grasses hissed in the breeze. The carpet hummed beneath Ermin's feet like a swarm of bees. She jammed her glasses onto the bridge of her nose. She could do this.

"I don't want to alarm anyone," said Georgie, "but Matron's heading this way."

"What?" Ermin jerked around. The carpet spun around in a dizzying circle. She brought it to a halt by leaning in the oppo-site direction. Sensing her prey, Matron leaned forward, urging on her flying doormat. Ermin dropped into a rider's crouch and leaned forward too. The carpet bolted like a wild horse. It jumped over the fence and careened down Lake Street, disturbing the sedate flight of a group of night clerks on hall runners. Several of the clerks shook raised fists at them. Ermin gave an experimental hop. The carpet lifted into the sky and left Matron far behind.

"All right?" she called out.

"Yes, fine." Colin's voice was pitched unusually high.

"Noooo..." Georgie moaned. There was a retching sound.

"Don't look down," Colin advised. "Eyes on the horizon."

Ermin did look down. Moonlight frosted the courthouse, the jail, and the Council's meeting house with its pink granite steps, making them look like giant, sugar-dusted cakes. She'd never been up this high before. The whole settlement lay spread out beneath her. For the first time, she could really see how everything connected. She leaned forward, urging the carpet on. They flew along the shores of Lake Georgina, a lake so large, everyone called it the Great Lake.

"Do you realize what this means?" Colin shouted. "We've escaped! We've got our own flying carpet. We can go anywhere! Do anything!"

"Not with winter coming on," said Ermin. "We've got no supplies."

A convoy of knackers rumbled into the yard of the Georgina Glue Factory, where haulers waited to unload the grisly cargo of dead cows and horses. Just east of the glue works, Commissioner George Savage had nailed yet another poster to the wall of the customs office—a revised likeness of Fisty Montgomery, no doubt. The poster kept changing because nobody knew what the elusive smuggler looked like.

"We could join Fisty's gang," said Colin. He'd seen the poster too.

"How are we supposed to find him? Nobody knows what he looks like and he lives on an uncharted island."

"By his flying canoe, of course. Everyone knows he's got one."

"Then he'd hardly go flying about in it, would he? It would be as good as telling everybody who he is."

"Do you have any better ideas? We can't go back to St. Anselm's. So where else can we go?"

That was the question. Scattered farms stretched northward. The sun lamps the farmers had wheeled onto the fields glowed as if on fire. Beyond the lamplit fields lay the rocky borderlands known as the Scrawlings. The rocks and boulders gave way to endless forest—the treaty boundary set by the Forest People to keep settlers contained within their leasehold.

"The forest?" she suggested.

"We can't cross the boundary without permission from the Forest People," said Georgie, who'd apparently recovered. "So we may as well head for our old den—and don't bother saying that someone else has taken it, Ermin. We still know how to fight... with or without conjurements."

They'd nearly reached the western border of Garrison Creek. Ahead lay the Magistrates' Fortress, its four black stone towers scraping the low-lying clouds. A black storm wand rose like a needle from the middle of the courtyard. Its fearful symmetry gave Ermin a jolt. She turned the carpet around and headed inland.

They didn't have to fight for a place under Crooked Mile Bridge. Their old den was entirely unoccupied and it was easy to see why. Waves dashed against the pilings, sending a fine spray of mist into the air. She and Colin had likened the Crooked Mile Bridge to a palace when, at seven years old, they'd first found it. Now, as she lay shivering beneath the carpet, she thought of her old bed at St. Anselm's. The dormitories had been drafty, but at least they'd been dry.

The next morning, their aching bellies forced them to comb through the refuse grounds behind St. Andrew's market, where they fought with other street kids for the grocers' castoffs. Ermin thought longingly of the gray, gluey porridge at St. Anselm's. Her daydreaming made her slow. A tiny girl pushed in front of her, grabbing a loaf of bread dotted with mold.

"Leave it!" Ermin swatted her away.

The girl stood back, her chest heaving. Ermin had a sudden vision of herself at the same age, weeping with hunger as the other, bigger children took all the food. This little girl didn't weep but regarded Ermin through large brown eyes—eyes that were far too large for her wizened face.

Ermin broke the loaf in two and tossed half of it to the girl. "Quit your gawking and run before the others see what you've got."

The girl flashed her a mouthful of crooked teeth and ran away.

"You'd better watch it," Georgie teased, "or you'll get a reputation for being soft. Cheer up. I've got us some cheese, though it's covered in sawdust, and Colin's scored us some bruised apples. We'll have breakfast yet!"

"We'd better eat on the move," said Colin. "We're new faces around here. Word's bound to get around."

They walked back to their den. The deactivated carpet sat lifelessly on Ermin's shoulders. She'd draped it over herself like one of Miss Fetchkeep's capes and secured it about her neck with the mooring rope. Just feeling it there gave her a surge of power.

"I think we should petition the Forest People for help," said Colin. "Some say their healers can even cure tree fever. Maybe if our parents had gone there in the first place, we wouldn't be orphans."

Whenever Ermin tried to remember her mother, all she saw were fragments of a face, like fallen leaves frozen in ice.

"It's not their fault," said Georgie. "Nobody knew much about tree fever then."

"Well, they should have known! They were our parents. Aren't adults supposed to know things?"

"My father was too drunk to know much of anything," said Georgie. "I know more than he ever did. I've always had to.

The three of us together know as much as any adult, maybe more."

Colin's face brightened. Trust Georgie to cheer him up!

The Crooked Mile den was just as empty as they'd left it. Ermin's sense of relief melted as they stowed themselves between the damp wooden pilings of the wharf. They'd have to find a better place, and soon. The winter storm swells would soon flood the beach with ice.

"We can't stay here much longer," said Georgie, echoing Ermin's thoughts.

"Let's go to the forest, like I said earlier," said Colin.

"We'd have to have something to offer them," said Georgie.

"We're wizards, aren't we?"

"They have their own wizards. We need something to sell."

Ermin's hand flew to her neck, but Miss Fetchkeep's necklace was still on the hook where she'd left it. Without access to her workshop, Ermin couldn't retrieve it, her accounts book, or even her messages—keys to running a profitable business. Without the ability to trade and bargain for supplies, how would they survive the winter? The question seized her like a rip current, pulling her thoughts into unknown depths.

"There's only one thing we can do," said Georgie. "We've got to find the Resistance."

"Do you think they'll take us in?" Colin asked.

"We're wizards, aren't we?"

"I'm not a wizard," said Ermin. "Why should they take me in?"

"Because you're our friend," said Georgie. "And you fix things. Wizards are notoriously bad at fixing things."

Ermin didn't rate her chances of fitting in as very high without knowing a few spells—the same spells she'd failed to calculate on her apprenticeship exam. Yet what was the alternative? They were on the run, they had no supplies, and every visit to the refuse fields to scrounge for food risked getting them captured by a gang. Ermin felt as if she'd gone around in a circle, ending up as homeless and helpless as she'd started. Georgie and Colin were looking expectantly at her.

"All right." It's not like she had anything better to suggest. Too bad they didn't know where Fisty's hideout was located. With her skills, she might be able to persuade someone to take her on as an apprentice. She gave a quiet, rueful laugh. If wishes were wings, then people might fly. She already could fly, though she hadn't yet found a place to land.

"It's all settled!" Georgie rubbed her hands together in glee. "We'll start our search at the drop-off spot where I last delivered the cards."

They set off on foot toward Old Town. They could have flown on the carpet, but it would have looked odd for three kids —two in St. Anselm's garb and one wearing worn, second-hand clothes—to be in possession of something so costly. Colin and Georgie pulled ahead, chattering away animatedly to each other while Ermin trailed along behind and tried not to think about much of anything at all.

Their route took them through the poorest section of Old Town, known as Pennyluck Place, a collection of ancient cabins and lean-tos so crooked and run down it was amazing they were still standing. Newly arrived immigrants and Faelings crowded into shelters too small for their extended families. Gaming dens, pawnshops, and old clothes stalls were the only businesses that prospered in this part of town—and not by much, judging from the dingy storefronts. Cellar taverns and smoking dens were common. Through a fringed curtain, Ermin caught a glimpse of shadowed bodies sprawled on the floor, their faces rimmed by a haze of sweet-smelling smoke. Beggars stumped up and down on mismatched crutches.

"I'd forgotten how bad this place is," Colin muttered.

Ermin didn't answer. In her mind's eye, she saw a bare room, a straw pallet with thin sheets. Four masked figures carried a shrouded form down the stairs to the death cart waiting in the street. She'd forgotten what her mother's face looked like, but not the wrenching terror of being left alone in that room. It was the day she'd first met Colin—the day they'd both been snatched.

Georgie stopped in front of the entrance to a courtyard, surrounded on three sides by grimy bricks. "It's just down here."

Instinctively, Ermin backed away. "I don't think so."

"It's not dangerous, just private," Georgie reassured her.

"Just the same, I'd rather keep watch." The courtyard felt too much like a trap.

"Me too," said Colin.

"Suit yourselves," said Georgie. She passed through the brick archway.

"She's either brave or crazy or both," muttered Colin.

"She's not crazy," said Ermin. Just desperate, like the rest of them.

Georgie re-emerged a short time later. "Nothing to find. There was always a note waiting before when I made the deliveries, but I guess since the deliveries stopped... Wait a minute. Isn't that Sclaw?"

Ermin whirled about. "Where?"

"Over there." Georgie jerked her chin at a familiar figure coming quickly up the street. Sclaw's wings were obscured by a brown paisley shawl, but there was no mistaking the scrape of her talons.

Georgie cowered behind them. "Stand in front of me,

would you? She doesn't like me very much. She's... rather protective."

"Of your darling Essey, you mean." Colin pursed his lips and made a loud kissing noise.

"Shut up!"

Ermin grinned. "Come on, Georgie. We know you like her."

"I do not."

Going sweet on a person not only turned you into a blithering idiot but made you a liar as well. Ermin was glad to have escaped the affliction. Sclaw let herself into a small cottage halfway up the street. She gave no sign that she'd noticed them.

"We'll have to place an ad in the classifieds," said Georgie. "That's how I always sent messages when I worked for Rustman. Do you have any money?" Ermin and Colin both shook their heads. "Then we'll just have to stake out the courtyard."

"No," Ermin and Colin said in unison. The courtyard was in Slap Dasher territory.

"Getting pressed into a gang was bad enough the first time round," said Ermin. "I don't fancy repeating the experience. Let's get moving before we attract attention."

"Then we'll need money to place a classified ad," Georgie insisted as they started to walk. "It's the only way."

"Maybe Ermin could collect a favor," Colin suggested.

"I left my accounts book in the workshop," said Ermin. "Without it, any apprentice I approach will have the upper hand. I'll end up being cheated."

"What if we sell the carpet?" Georgie asked.

"Not on your life." There was no way Ermin was giving up the carpet. She'd fixed it and she'd keep it.

Georgie threw up her hands in frustration. "Then how are

we going to place an ad? Don't you want to find the Resistance?"

Ermin was in no hurry to find the Resistance, but she thought better of saying so out loud. Colin and Georgie would only challenge her to come up with a better idea. She sighed. "I'll ask Denny Lorde. Maybe he'll help us. At least I can trust him." Being in debt to Denny wouldn't be as bad as it would be with some of the others.

They passed by the little cottage Sclaw had entered. Although it was as old as others on the street, someone (Sclaw?) had scrubbed the walls clean of mildew. There were no missing tiles on the roof. In fact, one or two of the slates had been replaced recently. Flower boxes rested on the windowsills, each one filled with glowbushes. The thick glass windows were steamed up from the leaves' radiant heat. The clippings from those bushes alone could easily heat a small cottage throughout the winter. That nobody had stolen them was a testament to Sclaw's fearsome reputation. Ermin didn't blame Georgie for being scared of her.

She caught a quick flicker of white cloth, as if one of the curtains had been disturbed, but when she looked back over her shoulder, the curtains were still. It might have just been her imagination. Danger seemed to lurk everywhere.

St. Andrew's market was still busy, even at this late hour. Ermin watched the crowd for any sign of yellow and black— Wharf Rat colors. The main thing was to deny the Rats any opportunity to pounce. This could be achieved if they attached themselves to marks, staying far enough away to remain unnoticed by the mark while keeping close enough to fool any watching gang member into thinking that they belonged to somebody else.

Ermin followed a mark who wore a heavy brocaded cloak trimmed with rabbit fur. She was probably a merchant, newly wealthy judging from the ostentatious display of rings—one on each finger, including both thumbs. Georgie walked alongside a heavily laden donkey cart. Colin trudged behind a thin, dour man with a metal steam leg that hissed and chugged as he stumped along. They abandoned their marks once they were sure they weren't being followed, then ran all the way to the smithy where Denny Lorde worked. It was highly unusual to make a call without first being summoned, but Ermin was counting on Denny to make allowances for emergencies.

The smithy was full of steam and the loud clanging of hammers. John Smith stood at the forge, turning a long metal strip in the fire. For once, he wasn't drunk. Ermin watched as he pulled the red-hot metal out of the flames without a stumble or a stagger. He put the strip in a bending fork and used a scrolling wrench to tug it into the shape of a circle, perhaps for a wheel. With each pull, his arms rippled with muscle like the great knotted roots of an oak. Ermin wouldn't have liked to be on the receiving end of one of his blows.

Denny came around the corner, balancing two buckets of water on a yoke. He started when he saw Ermin but covered his surprise with a grunt as he set down the buckets and poured them into the cooling trough. He re-hooked the buckets and went back around the corner, as if he was going to fetch more water. Ermin and the others followed him.

"What are you doing here?" Denny set his buckets down with a thump.

"I need a favor." It was hard for Ermin to get the words out. She cursed herself for ever leaving the necklace and accounts book in her workshop.

Denny's furrowed brow relaxed. A knowing smile played about his lips. "A favor, is it?"

"We need an ad placed in the classifieds. Can you do it?"

"Well, now, that depends. What are you willing to trade for it?"

Ermin gritted her teeth. "Two weeks of repairs, on the house."

"What, aren't you going to record the transaction?" Denny started back in mock surprise. "Where's your book?" When Ermin didn't answer, his eyes narrowed. "So, they've found you out."

"Something like that."

"Give me your ad. I'll place it. What paper?"

Ermin hesitated, trying to think of all the names.

"The *Sentinel*," Georgie cut in.

Denny gave her a sharp glance. "What are you doing running about the streets at this hour, Georgie Scratch? Don't you have work to do?"

"Great!" Ermin interjected before Georgie could say anything. "Two weeks of repairs, on the house."

"Two months," Denny said promptly.

"Three weeks."

"Four."

"Deal."

They spat on the ground and bumped elbows. Ermin hesitated. Stealing a carpet from D'Arcy to save her friends was one thing. Making false promises to a friend was another.

"There's just one thing: I can't get my messages right now."

"How am I supposed to summon you?"

"I'll have to check in with you every few days. I'll repay my debt, I swear. It just might take me more time."

Denny's eyes narrowed to slits. Finally, he nodded. "Fair

enough. If you were planning on cheating me, you'd never have told me that. Still, I'll record it in my book." He took out a grimy sheet of foolscap and a pencil nub. "Nickname?"

Ermin thought for a minute. "Shadow Apprentice."

Denny let out a chuckle. "Good one! Two months of service…"

"One."

"Just wanted to see if you had your wits about you. One month of service for one ad. Sign here." Ermin hastily scribbled "Shadow Apprentice" above his pointing finger. "What's the ad to say?"

"Frida knits socks," said Georgie. "Two coppers per pair."

"Frida knits socks, two coppers per pair," Denny repeated. "That's a strange message, to be sure."

"Denny!" John Smith bellowed. "Where are you, you useless runt?"

"I've got to go." Denny picked up the buckets with a clatter. Ermin felt the brief warmth of his hand on her arm. "Watch yourself."

He was the one who needed to watch out. The two empty buckets on either end of the yoke would no doubt earn him several hard clouts.

Loud kissing noises broke out behind her. Ermin whirled about in shock. Were Colin and Georgie actually kissing? The two of them stood side by side with huge grins plastered over their faces. If they had been kissing, they weren't doing it now.

Colin clasped both hands to his chest and rolled his eyes skyward. "Watch yourself, Ermin, my darling!"

"I will, Denny, my love!" Georgie trilled.

"What are you two going on about?"

"Do we have to spell it out?" Georgie said. "Denny's gone sweet on you."

"He never has!" Ermin recoiled at the thought. "How would that happen?"

Colin and Georgie doubled over with laughter. Ermin marched swiftly away from the forge, her entire face aflame.

～

By the time they walked all the way back to St. Andrew's market, Ermin was starving. She was debating whether to take a detour to the refuse fields when Georgie tapped her shoulder and waved a loaf of bread in her face.

"Go on, take it. Nobody saw. I was careful—no conjurements. See?" Georgie waggled her fingers. There was no telltale purple glow.

"It's not really thieving," said Colin. "She only pilfered the stuff they were going to throw away at the end of the day." Given the rate he was stuffing bread into his mouth, he was still regenerating from the night before. Not a good sign.

She thought about refusing, but what was the difference between pilfering leftovers destined for the refuse fields and picking through the refuse fields? Only a couple hundred yards and a fight. "Thanks," she said, taking the bread.

The outer crust was hard to chew, but the insides were soft. She pulled out the soft insides and was about to discard the crusts when she thought better of it. Who knew where their next meal would come from? She tucked the crusts away into her coveralls for later.

Reflexively, she scanned the streets. That's when she noticed them: two young Wharf Rats sitting atop a barrel. They were so small that both of them could fit on the lid. The larger of the two wore a yellow calico dress with black cutoffs underneath and a holey sweater on top. The other one was almost swallowed by an oversized black peacoat. The Rats stared past Ermin and her friends with studied disinterest. *It must be the St. Anselm's uniforms*, Ermin thought. As long as they wore them, she and Colin looked like they belonged to the school.

She took the long way back to the kip, checking over her shoulder to see if they were being followed. Something thumped overhead. Ermin looked up at the eaves, her stomach churning with dread. It wasn't Rats but a ginger cat who peered down at her, taking her measure with one good eye.

Colin blew out a slow breath. "I thought it was Rats for sure." He hastily tucked his glowing fingers away. "Don't look at me like that! I'm not doing it on purpose. I can't always control what happens."

"That's for sure," said Georgie. "Remember that time you changed Queen Georgina's hair to snakes?"

That day—when Colin had aimed a bewitcher at the portrait of Queen Georgina hanging in the school entrance hall —was a day that Ermin would remember for the rest of her life. As soon as the spell hit, the Queen's hair had instantly turned to hissing snakes—real ones. The snakes had slithered out of the frame and down the wall, leaving the poor monarch bald. Miss Fetchkeep had had to send the portrait away for restoration.

"Remember that time when Mr. Pinch, the gardener, clouted you when you shot an entire row of cabbages straight into the air?" said Ermin.

"Ah yes, the pincers," Colin said fondly.

"I don't remember that," said Georgie.

"You were already gone," said Ermin. "As soon as Mr. Pinch hit Colin, a set of pincers grew from the end of his spade."

"They broke off as soon as they crunched down on his leg," said Colin.

"That's true, but the spade went on growling for days."

All three of them laughed. Crooked Mile Bridge was just up ahead. Ermin urged them into a run. The last thing she wanted was to come face to face with any Wharf Rats, especially when Colin was so depleted.

Chapter Seven

Ermin sat up with a gasp. The kip was dark. Colin and Georgie lay curled around each other like puppies for warmth. Thunder rumbled across the lake. Waves pounded. Was it a flash of lightning that had woken her? Perhaps the packet of Speedwell's she'd tucked into her boot had pinched her foot.

Ermin patted the ground around them. Still dry. She was just about to lie down again when something rustled on the other side of the wall. They'd built a makeshift barrier out of some discarded logs and driftwood to keep the spray at bay. It couldn't be the Wharf Rats. They would have been put off by the St. Anselm's smocks and coveralls.

Only you're not at the school, are you? a disquieting inner voice whispered.

Ermin slowly stood up. A light clicked on, illuminating a face with bared, blackened teeth. She shouted in fear. Colin and Georgie scrambled to their feet, blinking and disoriented.

"Hello, hello. What have we here?" said the face, which

belonged to a boy with a yellow-and-black-checked scarf knotted around his neck.

Ermin knew what Colin and Georgie were going to do almost before they did it. She seized Colin's bewitcher, pointing it at the boy. The boy went flying backward, pursued by clouds of silvery-pink and lilac smoke.

"To the beach!" Ermin cried, slipping the carpet over her head while she ran. There was no time to retrieve her tool belt.

A crack of lightning illuminated a long line of figures spread out on the beach before them.

"Nab them!" yelled the boy with the checked scarf.

The line rushed them. Ermin smashed her fist against the activator button. Instantly, the carpet rose to a hover. How her feet found the steer straps so quickly, she didn't know. She lowered into a crouch and shot straight at the boy. He dropped to the sand with a cry of fright. Ermin banked and came around just as Georgie fired off a conjurement. Colin aimed the bewitcher at exactly the same time. In the flash of lightning that lit up the sky, a cloud of lilac-tinged smoke could be plainly seen. At least the conjurement hit the Wharf Rats. They froze in mid-run and toppled over, motionless. Ermin sped toward Colin and Georgie. They threw themselves onto the carpet. Ermin didn't dare wait for them to strap in their feet before she took off.

Shaken, they said nothing while they flew. Ermin headed west along the lake and touched down in a quiet residential area called the Annex, halfway between Old Town and New Town.

"Do you have anything to eat?" Georgie's voice was faint, her skin ashy.

Blowback.

Ermin patted her pockets, cursing herself for having eaten the whole loaf of bread Georgie had given her, before she remembered she'd saved the crusts. "I've got these. It's not much."

Georgie devoured the crusts. Ermin was furious with herself. She should have done more to help, starting with snatching more of that day-old bread when they'd had the chance. Her seven-year-old self wouldn't have hesitated. Denny was right. She was soft and out of practice, two qualities that spelled disaster on the streets. Out here, thieving was something you did for survival. It was wrong, no question, but with Georgie threatening to fall into a blowback-induced coma, "right" was a luxury she couldn't afford.

"We're going to get ourselves some proper food," she declared. Colin and Georgie flashed her puzzled looks. "Not from the refuse fields either. It's time we did some real picking. Georgie, Colin, you wait here."

"Okay, fine." That Georgie gave in without an argument was a sign of how depleted she really was.

"I'm not as bad as Georgie," said Colin. "I'll come with you."

Ermin looked at him doubtfully. Even if that was true, it wouldn't last.

"I'll make sure I eat the first thing I pilfer. It'll be okay."

"All right." Ermin knew better than to waste time arguing. Once Colin had made up his mind, he wouldn't budge. *Wizards. Always so stubborn!*

Ermin and Colin set off. Neighborhoods like this one always had small twenty-four-hour markets tucked away between the houses. In fact, there was one just up ahead.

"Do you want to play decoy or should I?" Ermin asked.

"I'll do it," Colin volunteered. He went inside.

Ermin watched through the window as he walked slowly around the store. The shopkeeper's suspicious gaze tracked his every move. Once she was sure that the shopkeeper was well and truly distracted, Ermin filled her pockets with apples and day-old rusks from the baskets out front. She took off at a brisk walk without waiting for Colin. Georgie was still at the corner where they'd left her. Ermin opened her smock to show her the haul.

Georgie let out a moan. "Ermin, you're the best." She pounced on the food. Colin arrived out of breath, having been chased out of the shop by the shopkeeper. His blowback was now clearly visible in the paleness of his skin and his unsteady steps. He devoured the rest of the food gratefully. Ermin waited for them to regain some strength before pushing on.

"You two are the only good things to ever have come out of St. Anselm's," Georgie said when she could speak. "My only true friends."

Ermin was surprised. "But you had lots of friends."

Georgie shook her head. "Not really. I was just good at hanging around the edges of groups, going along to get along. Thanks to Miss Fetchkeep, the other kids didn't really like me."

"Miss Fetchkeep? What did she do?"

"It was more about what she didn't do. I got great marks in writing, but I was never selected to help run the school paper."

"I didn't know we had a school paper," said Colin.

"It folded after a few issues," said Georgie. "It was so boring, nobody wanted to read it. I wanted to write for it, but Miss Fetchkeep wouldn't let me. Then there was that story contest, the one that Karen Shepard won."

"Your story should have won," said Ermin. "It was way better."

"I thought so too! Yet when I complained to Miss Fetch-keep, she lectured me on the importance of 'knowing my place.' The next thing I knew, I was packed off to old Rustman's shop. He was almost as racist as Miss Fetchkeep."

Ermin was so shocked, she stopped walking.

"What, you don't believe me?" Georgie mocked her.

"No, I do. It's just... I never noticed."

"Of course you never noticed! You're white. Or maybe you didn't want to notice because of the workshop she gave you."

Ermin flushed. Had she really been so clueless? It was true that she'd been grateful for Miss Fetchkeep's help and even felt beholden to her. It was unsettling to think that Miss Fetchkeep was not who Ermin thought she was, and even worse to find out that she'd targeted Georgie.

"Why didn't you tell us?" Ermin asked.

"What could you have done?"

"Nothing, I guess."

"That's why."

They came to a street of single-story cottages inhabited by weavers, spinners, carpenters, and shoemakers, who produced finished goods in their homes. The whitewashed walls of the cottages gleamed and the window boxes were filled with flowers. There was even a small machine shop. Ermin had always dreamed of working in a place like this. Now the dream was so close she could touch it, yet at the same time, it was farther away than ever. A hopeless yearning filled her, as if she'd become a kind of ghost, pressing against the window of a life she could never have.

A three-noted trill sounded from above. A chorus of similar cries echoed around them. Before Ermin had time to react, a Wharf Rat shimmied down a drainpipe into the street. Only one, tiny, wearing a too-big peacoat. Even Ermin could handle one Rat. She started toward him. The tiny Rat whirled. A gap in the coat revealed that he wore only a ragged pair of shorts underneath. His bare legs were blue with cold. She hesitated. Peacoat threw back his head and let out another trill—a big sound for such a small boy. Boots clattered on the tiles overhead.

Sparks of red flew from Colin's fingers as he waved his hands to ignite rows of red winter poppies in the window boxes. The flowers writhed into vines, red-toothed maws snapping at everything in sight.

Ermin ducked as a needle-toothed bloom reared up on her right. Another conjurement sprayed from Colin's wrist nozzle and landed on a snarling poppy. The flower detached itself from its stem and sprouted legs, startling a sleeping cat. Wharf Rats who'd started to shimmy down the drainpipes now scrabbled back up in an attempt to escape the monster flowers. The commotion drew several people out of their cottages.

Ermin lunged for Colin, but it was too late. A cloud of pink-tinged smoke wafted toward a row of moon cabbages. They rose up, their outer leaves transformed into whirling blades. One of the bladed cabbages flew toward the tiny Rat, who was hovering near a privy. Ermin pushed him out of the way. The cabbage exploded against the privy's wall in a rain of coleslaw. One of the blades broke off, narrowly missing the side of her head.

"You all right?" she asked the child.

A muzzle poked into her back.

"Hands behind your back, real easy like," said a voice behind her.

Reluctantly, she obeyed. Her arms were grabbed and twisted. Two cold circles closed around her wrists with a metallic click. The carpet was ripped from her shoulders. She knew better than to call out to the watching cottagers for help. Nobody meddled in Wharf Rat business. Besides, they were too busy doing battle with the walking flowers.

She was spun around and came face to face with the same dead-eyed girl she'd seen perched atop a barrel with Peacoat. Only this time the girl's gaze was bright and alert. Measuring.

Three other Rats stepped up. One held the carpet while

the other two jostled Georgie and Colin along in front of them, their wrists bound with metal bands. Their faces sagged with fatigue. Iron had a deadening effect on wizards, which was why it was so favored by the Magistrates, but it was far too expensive for street gangs. How had the Rats gotten hold of Magistrates' cuffs?

"What a haul!" crowed Colin's captor. "Better roll up that carpet before Chaser gets here. You know how he is. You were right about their den, Snarl. It was exactly where you said."

The girl who'd cuffed Ermin stuffed the carpet into a backpack she was carrying. From it, she pulled out a miniature telescopic lens and handed it to Peacoat. "Up you go, Mouse. See if you can find out what's happened to the others."

"Righto." Peacoat scampered up the drainpipe as nimbly as a squirrel.

Their indifference yesterday had been an act, meant to disarm her. Snarl had obviously followed their progress from the roofs as they'd made their way to the den, then planned the ambush. Ermin might as well have dropped a trail of pebbles to mark the way.

Peacoat peered over the edge of the roof. "Chaser's coming."

A few moments later, the same stringy-haired boy Ermin had flattened with her carpet appeared. He strode toward them, fists clenched, with murder in his eyes. "I don't care what Rory said, I'm going to kill them."

Snarl stepped in front of him, but Chaser shoved her out of the way. He grabbed a fistful of Ermin's smock and jerked her forward until she was inches from his face. "From all the fuss Rory makes about you, anybody would think you're special, but I bet you're not feeling so special right now, are you?"

He shoved Ermin face first into the wall of the nearest cabin. She turned her head sideways just in time to keep her nose from being smashed. Chaser planted his forearm into the base of her neck, his foul breath hot against her ear. With his other hand, he groped her.

"Stop it, Chaser!" Snarl's voice was sharp.

Chaser whirled. The pressure on Ermin's neck lessened. She gasped for breath. "I'm squad leader. I can do whatever I want. It's thanks to me we've reeled in this quarry."

"Snarl's the one who found them," Mouse corrected him.

Chaser let go of Ermin and backhanded him across the face. Mouse's neck snapped back so violently, Ermin was sure he'd broken it. Snarl pulled Mouse out of the way before Chaser could strike again. She planted herself in front of Ermin, effectively blocking her from Chaser's wrath.

"Remember what Rory said? He wants the St. Anselm's captures whole and unharmed."

"I know what he said!" Chaser swung around to face the circle of silent Rats. "I found the den, I planned the ambush. Got it? If anyone says any different, they'll get a lot worse than the back of my hand. Give me that bewitcher!"

A Rat came forward with Colin's bewitcher. Chaser wrenched it away. He flexed the wrist hose before throwing the bewitcher to the ground. "Piece of junk. Anything else?"

Nobody said a word about the carpet.

Ermin sent up a silent thanks that she'd tucked the Speed-well's away in her boot. She could feel the packet if she flexed her foot, safe and sound.

"Blindfold them."

Snarl tore off her scarf and wrapped it around Ermin's head. The already dim daylight muted before a suffocating black curtain. Ermin tried not to gag as she breathed in the sour, unwashed smell of the cloth. She tried looking down but couldn't see much beyond the scuffed toes of her boots.

"Try anything and I'll nail you," Chaser warned.

He needn't have worried. Iron-bound, there was nothing they could do. Yet.

Vision was reduced to a very thin line at the edge of the blindfold. Ermin kept her gaze fixed on her boots. There was a good chance they were being taken to the Wharf Rats' current headquarters. If she paid attention to the ground beneath her feet, she might be able to map out its location. The cobblestones changed to muddy ruts as they left the Annex. Ermin had no idea what direction they were heading in. She focused on putting one foot in front of the other, all of her senses on high alert. They walked for a long time. Ermin had started to wonder if she was doomed to walk sightless forever, when the toe of her left boot stubbed against something hard. She stumbled. Snarl grabbed her elbow to steady her.

"Lift your feet," Snarl directed in a low voice, as if she didn't want the others to hear.

Ermin did as she was told. Below the scarf, wooden boards swam into view. A sidewalk. That meant they were west of the Old North Road, the street that divided Old Town from the far wealthier New Town to the west. Merchants and residents there had built wooden sidewalks in front of their shops and houses. They didn't exist anywhere else in the Creek. Ermin couldn't imagine the Rats hiding out in one of the swanky shops or a New Town mansion.

Snarl took her by the elbow again to guide her around a corner. The wooden sidewalk was replaced by another mud-soaked thoroughfare. She heard no government workers swishing by on their carpets, only the muffled clop of horses' hooves and the creak and groan of carts that heralded the early-morning arrival of farmers. There was no point in calling out for help. Most farmers paid protection money to the gangs in order to safely bring their goods to market. They wouldn't jeopardize their livelihoods for the sake of a few orphans.

Ermin kept her eyes fixed on the thin line of vision at the edge of the scarf. They clattered up one flight of steps and down another. Rose-colored granite glinted beneath her boots. Ermin felt a surge of triumph. Only the Council's meeting house had pink granite steps.

"Check her scarf," Chaser ordered. "She's keeping up with nary a stumble."

The scarf was jerked down over Ermin's mouth. Now it was almost impossible to breathe, let alone see. Her foot came down on empty air. Hands gripped her body to steady her.

"Watch yourself." Snarl's voice was barely a whisper in her ear. "These steps are uneven."

Ermin almost found herself liking her. Chaser likely would have booted Ermin down the steps.

The air grew chill, smelling of mold and lake water. Pressed by the blindfold, Ermin's eyes ached. She couldn't judge how far they'd gone or how long they'd been walking. All sense of time and distance dissolved in the total blackness. She was relieved when the ground finally leveled out. Snarl kept hold of her elbow. The path underfoot grew slick and treacherous with protruding stones. After a while, she pulled Ermin to a stop.

Chaser's voice pierced the silence. "Lower the plank." His words echoed slightly. Metal hinges creaked. Chains rattled. These sounds created more echoes that bounced back from distant walls.

"We'll have to lift them across," said a Rat.

"Don't touch me!" Colin's voice rang out.

"Shut up!"

Hands hooked beneath Ermin's armpits, hoisting her up and through the air before setting her down on her feet again. Her boots thudded against wooden planks that rocked to and fro in a steady rhythm. If she didn't know any better, she'd have thought she was standing on the deck of a ship, but the moldering air smelled more like a cellar.

Chaser let out a satisfied breath. "Home sweet home!"

"Our very own *Lucky Charm*," added one of the Rats.

The *Lucky Charm* was the boat that had carried the original immigrants to their new settlement. For years, it had languished in the harbor, its rotting hulk used as a coffin ship to house dying tree fever victims. Misery had clung to it like a ghostly miasma. Ermin had been among those who had cheered when it sank in a gale last November. How could she be standing on its deck?

A slap echoed in the silence, followed by a frightened squeak. "Go and fetch the boss before I rip that yammer right out of your gob!" Chaser barked.

Ermin's hands clenched into fists. Her feet itched to plant kicks on Chaser's shins and backside. She was more determined than ever to escape, Rory or no Rory.

Unsteady footsteps scuttled away. The creaky groan of ropes was added to the steady slap of water. It certainly sounded like a ship. Ermin flexed her wrists, straining against the manacles, but they wouldn't budge. Top-grade gear, this. Again, she wondered how the Rats had managed to get their greasy paws on it.

Heavy boots advanced across the deck with a slow menace. Ermin's skin crawled.

"Take off their blindfolds," a deep voice said.

The suffocating scarf was torn away. Ermin blinked as her surroundings came into focus in the dim light. She was indeed standing on the deck of a ship more than a hundred feet long. Replacing the sky overhead was a high rock ceiling studded with stalactites the color of frosted plums. Yellow-green glow rocks were set into the walls at intervals, as though they'd been purposely stuck there to be used as lights. The entire ship had come to rest inside a giant cave. Georgie and Colin stood stunned and speechless beside her.

The *Lucky Charm*.

Underground.

A grimy face filled her vision and grinned, showing two sharp front teeth fused together like a rat's. "It's so good to have you home at last."

Ermin recoiled. It was Rory Smythe, King of the Rats. He was dressed in a yellow-checked topcoat and tails and wore a pair of silver-toed boots. He touched his black top hat in a mock salute. "I've been so looking forward to this little reunion."

"You can't touch us," said Ermin. "We're wearing St. Anselm's colors, and Georgie's apprenticed." It was foolhardy to talk back to the Rat King, but she was desperate enough to try to bluff her way out.

"We'll see if her master wants to buy her back, then. As for you, you've left St. Anselm's, haven't you? Otherwise, you'd never have been caught sleeping under Crooked Mile Bridge. The only question is: Why?" Rory tapped his fused teeth thoughtfully. "You were safe at the school, weren't you? Warm and fed. You left all that behind, and for what? I think I can guess."

Ermin went cold. What had Rory guessed?

Rory turned to Chaser. "Did you find anything on them?"

"Only an old bewitcher. It was a piece of junk, so I threw it away."

For the first time, Ermin felt almost glad that he had. If Rory had taken the bewitcher apart, it might have confirmed his suspicions. Why else would scrubbers have been installed inside the spell shaft? Maybe Colin's and Georgie's secret was still safe.

Rory's eyes narrowed. "It's not your job to make decisions, is it? Take them down below."

"Aren't we going to get anything for them? You said the St. Anselm's ones were special." Chaser stood his ground, whether from bravery or stupidity, Ermin didn't know. The other Rats backed away from him. "You said that whoever found them would get a reward."

"I don't recall saying anything like that." Rory took a step forward, cocking his head to one side. "Do you, Rats?"

"No, Rory," the assembled Rats chorused.

"That's what I thought. Snarl!"

Snarl stepped forward. "Yes, Rory?" She was as skinny and ragged as the rest of the gang, but her air of alert calm offered a striking contrast to Chaser's bully-boy bluster and Rory's smirking cruelty. Ermin would have liked her for a friend if Snarl wasn't a Rat.

Rory turned to Chaser. "See, that's what I like. Respect and obedience. Remember that when you stuff your hands into your pockets tonight and find them empty. How old are you, Snarl?"

"Eleven."

Rory's amber eyes flicked up and down Snarl's body. "Not quite old enough for Madame Violet's. In another year or two, maybe, but not yet. You can be squad leader... for now."

"Yes, Rory."

"But... but... " Chaser sputtered.

Rory inspected his nails, which were long and filthy. "Yes, Chaser? You have something to say?"

One of the other Rats elbowed the gormless Chaser into silence.

"That's what I thought. Snarl, take the captives downstairs and put them in the holding pen. Chaser, you'll be swabbing the decks...alone."

Snarl took Ermin by the elbow and pushed her into a line behind Colin and Georgie. She tied them all together with a length of rope, a graphic reminder of their press gang status. "Let's go."

When Ermin drew level with Rory, his lips drew back from his teeth, more a baring of fangs than a smile. He reached out as if to chuck Ermin under the chin but pressed one filed claw to her throat instead. "I'll get what I'm owed, one way or another. You can be sure of that."

Chapter Eight

Snarl ushered Ermin, Colin, and Georgie down a narrow hatchway into the ship's hold. A few yellow glow rocks had been hammered into the walls here too. Rows of empty hammocks hung across their path like giant cobwebs. Snarl batted them aside. Ermin recognized her old hammock now swinging a few yards away from the brig, a square cage formed from bars bolted into the ceiling and floor. The combined smells of mildewed wood and unwashed bodies were beyond foul. Bilge water sloshed around in unseen gutters. Tiny feet pattered in the shadows. *Rats.* Real ones.

Snarl ushered them inside the empty brig and slammed the door. She retreated down the corridor. Mouse stared at them through the bars, shifting from one foot to another until Snarl returned, bearing three steaming bowls on a tray. She handed the tray to Mouse while she unlocked the cell door. Mouse set down the tray and shoved it toward them.

"How are we supposed to eat with our hands behind our backs?" Ermin asked.

Snarl unstrapped a cattle prod from her belt and handed it to Mouse. "If they move, zap them."

Mouse hefted the cattle prod. It was almost as big as he was. Snarl swiftly unlocked all three sets of manacles and retreated. The cell door fell to with a clang.

Georgie and Colin fell on the bowls like two starving dogs. Ermin recoiled. The gruel smelled like an Old Town dust heap during a heat wave.

"What's the matter?" Snarl asked. "Not hungry?"

Ermin didn't reply. Nothing would induce her to swallow a single mouthful of that slop. Besides, Colin and Georgie needed it more. They could divvy up her share.

"It tastes better than it smells." Snarl paused as if she was going to say something else, but she clapped Mouse on the shoulder. "Come on. Let's go."

She and Mouse moved off. The hatch door clanged back into place. The metal bolt slammed shut.

Ermin thought of the tool pouch she'd abandoned back at the den. What she wouldn't give for her lock picks now! At least the Speedwell's were safe. She leaned her forearms against the bars and pushed, testing for weakness.

"Ouch!"

Something had pricked her arm. She held up her sleeve, the one with the rip. The fastening pin had popped open, exposing its sharp point. Ermin grinned. It looked like she didn't need the lock picks after all.

She bent the fastening pin back and forth until it broke into two pieces. She bent one of the pieces into an into an L shape, folding one end back on itself to create a thicker piece. The other piece of the pin she left straight. Snarl had fastened the cell door with a plain, ordinary padlock. Perfect.

Ermin inserted the thick L end into the bottom of the keyhole. She turned the wrench clockwise, then counterclockwise. On the counterclockwise turn, the pressure lessened. The lock turned left.

"Aren't you going to eat?" Colin asked.

"You can have it. I'm not hungry." Ermin's stomach rumbled as she spoke.

There was a small silence.

"We'll go halves," said Colin. "Georgie, give me your bowl."

Ermin inserted the straight pin—the pick—into the upper part of the keyhole, pushing it back while keeping pressure on the L-shaped piece—or torque wrench—below. She had to be careful. If she applied too much pressure, the wrench would snap. Too little, and she wouldn't be able to pick the lock. She jiggled the straight piece upward to depress the pins. She felt one of them give. Keeping pressure on the torque wrench, she inserted the pick again and located the three remaining pins. She depressed them, one by one. She gave the torque wrench one final twist counterclockwise. The padlock sprang open.

"You're a crack lock pick," Georgie said with a tinge of envy.

Ermin swung the cage door shut behind them and refastened the lock, not knowing what to say. If she agreed, she'd sound arrogant. If she protested, she'd be lying.

"She had a lot of practice at St. Anselm's," said Colin. "I thought she might even open another business on the side. Listen, that small Rat who helped snatch us never came up to the deck while Rory was talking. I have an idea he might have stowed the carpet somewhere, like in one of the hammocks."

"I bet you're right." If Ermin had stolen contraband she didn't want Rory to know about, she would have stowed it in her hammock as well. A carpet could easily be disguised as a blanket, particularly one as beat up as theirs.

"I'll keep watch over the hatch," Georgie offered.

Ermin and Colin combed through the hammocks, checking

the storage trunks as well as the gutters. Nothing. Where else could they have hidden it? Emptied of cargo, the hull was a vast, echoing space. Another hatchway led down to the lowest section of the ship—the bilge.

Colin eyed the hatch in horror. "We're not going down there?"

"It's the only place left to look."

Squeaks drifted up through the hatch, along with the back-and-forth slosh of water. A fetid mixture of rotting fish, dank fur, and excrement combined in a stink so foul, it was madness to think of going down there. That's also what made it the perfect hiding place.

"I'm too tired to conjure up a light."

"Let's pry off some of those glow rocks instead."

Hands full of rocks, Ermin and Colin shone them into the bilge's depths. Dark water speckled with tiny red dots reflected the light at them. The bilge was full of rats.

Colin jerked back convulsively, dropping one of the rocks. It landed with a soft thud, no splash. That was odd. Ermin stuck her head down through the hatch and shone a light on its underside. She saw the carpet almost immediately, parked in a hover with its mooring rope thrown over a beam. On the carpet sat a tiny figure in a peacoat.

"Mouse!"

"Snarl thought that nobody would find it here," said Mouse. "But I thought that you might. Is it true that you once escaped from Rory?"

"We escaped from him, all right," Colin assured him. "And we're about to do it again. Now, hand over that carpet."

"No." Mouse folded his arms across his chest. "It's our carpet now. Mine and Snarl's."

"You little weasel!" Colin sputtered.

Ermin suppressed a smile. Mouse couldn't have been more

than five years old. Yet here he was, already standing his ground like a seasoned scrapper. "What if we tell Rory you've hidden the carpet from him? Go on, Colin. Bang on the grate and shout for Rory."

"No!" Mouse cried.

"Then you'd best throw me the end of that rope."

"Are you going to leave us?"

"Throw us the rope. Then we'll talk."

Mouse pulled the rope over the beam and tossed the loose end to her. She caught it. "Thanks."

Mouse watched solemnly as she hauled the carpet over. "You were never a Rat," he pronounced. "You're too nice."

"Not so nice that I won't inform on you if you double-cross us. Where's Snarl?"

"She told me to wait for her here. I'm so little, I can hide without being noticed," Mouse boasted.

"That's a good skill to have," said Ermin. Mouse's story confirmed that Snarl was planning on using the carpet to escape. Ermin didn't blame her. She'd have done exactly the same thing. Snarl and Mouse could have been an echo of herself and Colin plotting their getaway from the Rat King.

Colin must have been thinking something similar because he laid a hand on Mouse's shoulder as he began to climb off. "Stay put, in case we need to take off in a hurry."

A breathless Georgie appeared at their shoulder. If she was surprised to see Mouse, she didn't show it. She began to buckle his tiny feet into a set of passenger's straps while she jerked her thumb toward the ceiling—the signal for *up*. Colin jumped on. Ermin soared upward, grabbing a beam to stop them from colliding with the upper deck.

The grille to the upper deck clanged open. A pair of silver-toed boots appeared on the ladder, reflecting a milky-white light that came from a jellyfish imprisoned inside a jar. As the jellyfish contracted its bell, light pulsated through the glass. Quietly, Ermin passed her glow rocks to Georgie. Colin had some too. They could use them as missiles. Any second now, Rory would reach the empty cage. Then all fury would break loose.

For once, neither Georgie's nor Colin's fingertips glowed with wizardry. Their breakout would be done the old-fashioned way, without conjurements. Rory had left the metal grille wide open. The hatch was big enough to fly through—just. They'd have flown through right then if Snarl wasn't blocking the way, climbing down the ladder after Rory. When she reached the bottom, Rory's large hand clamped around her skinny wrist.

"What do you mean, she didn't eat? I told you to dose all three of them! That old blighter won't buy them unless they're knocked out cold." Rory dragged Snarl after him as he headed for the cage.

The way was clear. Ermin raised a questioning eyebrow at Colin and Georgie, jerking her head after Rory and Snarl. They both nodded in silent agreement: they'd save Snarl first. Curses rang out, magnified by the empty hull. Ermin pushed the carpet forward, using the beams, until Rory and Snarl came into view.

"Why did you take off their manacles, you stupid girl? Don't you know what they are?" Rory raised his hand to strike Snarl. "I'll beat you senseless."

Mouse cried out, but Georgie covered his mouth with her hand. Ermin dropped to her knees. The carpet shot downward, then leveled out as she rose to a half crouch. She doubted if Rory even saw them coming. He went flying. Ermin and Colin grabbed Snarl by the arms and hauled her onto the carpet.

"Guards!" Rory screamed. He made a sudden lunge for them but was beaten back by a shower of glow rocks.

Chaser and a couple of the older Rats stepped forward to block the exit, smacking wooden pegs against the grate. Ermin took a moment to line up the carpet. They only had one chance at this, and it would be a tight fit. Chaser and his fellow Rats had no idea how fast the carpet could go. It would be a pleasure to mow them down.

"Ready?" Ermin asked. Georgie and Colin crouched over Mouse and Snarl to hold them in place. "Now!" Ermin yelled.

She strained forward, hoping against hope that they weren't going to smash into the side of the hull. Like a shooting star, the carpet sped toward the open hatchway. Chaser and his cronies tried to block the exit but the carpet was too fast. It plowed straight through them. Their grabbing hands snatched at Ermin and she twisted, sending the carpet spinning upward. She leaned in the opposite direction for all she was worth, then dropped to her knees as a purplish-white stalactite grazed her cheek. The carpet dropped sharply. She rose to a half crouch to level out. Her heart hammered with panic and also with something else: excitement. They'd done it! They'd broken free of Rory for the second time!

Not quite.

Rats swarmed across the deck of the *Lucky Charm*. They slid down the gangplank, some of them on their bellies.

"They won't give up," warned Snarl. "Rory will skin them alive if they don't catch us."

"Which is the way out?" Ermin asked Snarl.

"Up ahead, to your left. There's a tunnel under that hanging curtain of moss. Hurry!"

Ermin leaned forward. Damp air whistled past her ears. Chaser was pounding down the path by the side of the boat. His mouth twisted into a snarl as he put on an extra burst of speed to intercept the runaways. Ermin urged the carpet forward into the mouth of the tunnel as fast as she dared. The carpet juddered as it shot through the curtain of moss, as if something had fallen on it. Ermin cast a worried glance over her shoulder. Colin and Georgie had toppled over, senseless. Snarl crouched between them, interlacing their arms with hers. "Keep going! It's the gruel—it was drugged. I won't let them fall."

Chaser had reached the mouth of the tunnel. Ermin had no choice but to keep flying. Mouse pitched the last of the glow rocks at their pursuers. Ermin heard the shouts as they hit.

"You'll hit the stairs after the next bend," said Snarl. "You'll want to angle up. The steps are all the same height. You can go faster if you keep to the same angle."

They rounded the bend. The steps came up suddenly. Without the warning, Ermin would have flown smack into them. Her thighs ached as she raised and lowered her crouch to maintain an even angle.

"They're gaining on us," said Snarl.

Ermin gritted her teeth. She was playing it too safe. She was going to have to risk more speed or they'd be captured. What Rory would do to them didn't bear thinking about. She leaned forward, planting her stance. Damp air raked at her face. Nobody spoke. Ermin could feel them all behind her, willing her to go on. Cold air siphoned down through the shaft —the smell of open space, of freedom. With one final surge of speed, they burst from the tunnel.

Wind enveloped her, smelling of fish and lake weed, whipping the hair away from her face. Congratulatory thumps landed on her back and shoulders. She shouted from pure exhilaration. She felt like a caged bird finally flying free.

"Is everybody all right?" Ermin called back over her shoulder.

"Aside from nearly getting brained by rocks, just fine," said Snarl. "How about you, Mouse?"

"So...much...fun!" Mouse gasped.

They all laughed as the carpet soared into the azure sky, clear for once.

Down below, waves churned and foamed over the rocks that marked the entrance to the cave. The Rats couldn't have tugged the *Lucky Charm* all the way from the harbor to the cave by themselves. They must have had help. On top of the cliff, the pale yellow bricks of the meeting house shone like a beacon. The stairs had led down to the cave from the meeting house above, stairs the Rats shouldn't have had access to. Someone powerful had let them in.

Chapter Nine

"I'm hungry."

Mouse's whisper carried in the quiet at the edge of the woods. It was so quiet, it seemed to Ermin as if the entire Scrawlings was holding its breath. The small fire they had built smoked and steamed. Most of the sticks they'd gathered were wet. It had been hard to find dry wood, but they didn't dare to venture any farther into the scrubby bush for fear of stirring up trouble. Bandits were always a problem in the Scrawlings.

"Well, we've got greens and tubers," Georgie said, having finally awoken from her drugged slumber along with Colin.

"What are we supposed to do with them—eat them raw?" Colin said.

"We could boil them if we had a good cooking basket," said Georgie. "Only trouble is, those take time to make."

"What good is putting a basket over an open fire?" Colin demanded. "It'll only go up in flames."

"We don't put it over the fire, Colin. We fill the basket with water and put hot stones inside it to make the water boil. Chunks of granite work best. They won't crack in the heat from the fire. We've got lots of stones but no basket."

"Does it have to be a basket?" Ermin asked.

"No, it could be anything. I remember my uncle once used an abandoned dugout canoe for a cook pot."

"What about a tree stump?"

"Show me."

Ermin led Georgie down to the river. She'd noticed the stump earlier when she'd gone to fetch water. It was half-hidden behind a massive fallen tree, slick with green moss and ridged with discs of fungus. The violence of the break was still apparent in the splintered tears that stuck up in sharp stakes around the stump's outer rim, but inside, the stump was hollow.

Georgie gave the stump an experimental scrape with her knife. "Looks like something's eaten it out, maybe ants, but the rim's still solid." She turned to Mouse, who had tagged along behind them. "Go back and put as many fist-sized rocks as you can in the fire to heat them up. We'll need some forked sticks too." She turned back to Ermin. "You know, this might work. Let's flood this stump. I don't know about you, but I don't fancy getting a mouthful of ants when I sit down to eat."

They flooded the stump. The ants either had left long ago or had been eaten by birds. Ermin stayed by the stump to chip away and scrape out the rotten bits while Georgie coached the others on the art of carrying hot stones with pairs of forked sticks. She and Snarl were the only ones who really excelled at this task. Colin's efforts were passable. When Ermin finished scraping out the stump she joined the stone-carriers, but she kept on dropping the stones. No matter what she did, she couldn't get the hang of it. Discouraged, she threw her sticks back into the fire.

Mouse, who'd not been allowed to carry a stone of his own, drifted away from Snarl's side. Maybe Ermin's ineptitude had convinced him she was to be pitied more than feared. "Why did you burn your sticks?"

"Because I hate them."

Mouse nodded as if this made perfect sense. "I can find you some new ones." He started for the bushes, but Ermin stopped him.

"No!" Earlier, she'd nearly tripped over a small skeleton curled up on its side at the edge of the woods. She didn't want him to stumble across anything so gruesome. Hurriedly, she added: "Do you know how to skip stones?"

Mouse's face lighted up. "Snarl says I'm the best skipper, even better than her."

"Can you show me?"

"Won't we get in trouble?"

"Nobody can tell us what to do out here. We're the bosses of ourselves."

"Me too?"

"You too."

Mouse flashed her a gap-toothed grin and slipped his hand into hers. It was such a tender, trusting gesture that Ermin was taken aback. Mouse seemed not to notice her awkwardness as he skipped beside her, chattering about how many rocks he could throw, and how far. Snarl gave Ermin a stiff nod as they passed, part relief and part warning, as if to tell her not to get too close. Although Ermin might be holding his hand, Mouse belonged to Snarl.

Ermin lay awake that night, peering at the night sky through the sticks of a makeshift lean-to. Each stick represented a separate worry. Take this lean-to, for starters. It barely worked to keep the rain off, and it would be woefully inadequate once the snows came. Any attempt to establish a more permanent camp might attract the attention of bandits, and she didn't fancy being pressed into service by bandits any more than by Rats. Next, food. They wouldn't be able to scrounge for greens and roots after the ground froze. If Colin and Georgie were forced to use conjurements, the lack of food would soon prove fatal. They had to find the Resistance, fast. How were they to do that without letting Snarl and Mouse in on their secret?

She must have slept because the next thing she knew, light was slanting in through the cracks and Colin was shaking her shoulder.

"Wake up, lazybones! You'll never guess who we've met." At Ermin's blank stare, he added, "Fisty's gang!"

"What?" Ermin sat bolt upright. A delicious smell of woodsmoke and frying fish wafted in on the air.

Colin grinned. "You can smell it, can't you? Hurry, or you'll be too late."

"Too late for what? Where is everybody?"

"They're already there. Hurry!"

Ermin's cold fingers made clumsy work of fastening the carpet's mooring rope around her neck. She was several yards behind Colin as he led the way down a trail of recently flattened grass.

"There's a piece of Snarl's yellow skirt tied to that branch," said Colin. "It's not far now."

They entered a strand of trees with an underskirt of cold shadow. After a minute or two, they came to a small clearing. Ermin spotted Georgie and Snarl at once, talking to two girls. Mouse was skipping stones at the water's edge. A woman clad in a sheepskin coat and armed with a cudgel tended to a catch of skewered fish hung over a fire. Another examined the bottom of an overturned canoe. If Ermin had come across these women by herself, she would have run. Everything about them, from their muscled legs and arms to their weapons, spelled *bandit*.

The woman tending the fire noticed her and lifted a hand in greeting. "Come and join us!"

Ermin hesitated. Nobody offered food for free without demanding something in return. What did they want?

The woman bent over the canoe straightened. "Don't stand there for too long or you might get stolen." Her dark brown face creased into laugh lines. Salt-and-pepper locs, loosely bundled together with a red and black ribbon, spilled down her back. Her wool cloak was pulled back over her shoulders to reveal an armored breastplate.

It looked as though her comrades had already been stolen, and happily so. If the bandits were intent on keeping them, there wasn't much they could do. Besides, the smell of frying fish was killing her. Warily, Ermin stepped forward.

The other woman snatched off her fleece cap, exposing a shaved head. She bent into a low bow. "Lieutenant Mehta Murthy, at your service."

"I'm Captain Spiria Coraleone," the woman by the canoe said. "These are our two apprentices, Lizzie and Myranda."

One of the apprentices was a pale ghost of a girl with spiked blond hair, though her muscles were wiry beneath her sheepskin vest. The other girl's jet-black hair was also spiked. Her eyes were ringed with gang markings—Slap Dasher, by the looks of it.

Every instinct told Ermin to run, but she couldn't leave her friends. Refusing the bandits' hospitality might anger them, so she sat down by the fire.

Lieutenant Murthy pried a fish off its skewer and laid it on top of a wet piece of birchbark. She handed it to Ermin. "Eat. Otherwise, Lizzie will have it all."

Ghost Girl bared her teeth in a smile. They'd all been filed to sharp points. Lizzie looked quite capable of devouring the fish and Ermin both. Ermin shoveled the tender pieces of fish into her mouth, skin and all.

"Any luck with that canoe yet?" Lieutenant Murthy asked.

Captain Coraleone's brow furrowed. "The keel's been ruptured. Without more flywood, we may have to travel the old-fashioned way—by paddle."

Ermin craned her neck for a better glimpse. The keel must be the raised ridge of wood that ran along the bottom. As Captain Coraleone had said, the back half of it had broken off.

"Good thing the keel took the blow rather than the hull," said Lieutenant Murthy.

"It'll take less work to fix," Captain Coraleone agreed.

Underneath the canoe sat a row of small kegs, half-covered by oilcloth. Captain Coraleone reached between them to pull out a blanket roll, then yanked the oilcloth down over the kegs to cover them. She began to unwrap the blanket roll. Inside was a collection of the most amazing tools that Ermin had ever seen. Some of them were old and worn, but all were clean, free of rust, and well oiled. Ermin gazed enviously upon the priceless riches on display.

"You've got a wood raveler!" she cried, recognizing the tool. It looked nothing like her cloth raveler. Instead of rotating hooks, there were retractable, sharp-edged discs for cutting and a stamper for sealing.

Captain Coraleone turned to her in surprise. "Not many would recognize a tool like that."

"Ermin would," Colin boasted. "She's the best mechanic in all of Garrison Creek."

"Colin!"

"Well, you are."

Captain Coraleone and Lieutenant Murthy exchanged a look. "Why don't you come over here and take a look at this boat?"

Ermin glared at Colin. *Blabbermouth.* She couldn't very well refuse since she'd already eaten their food. If she was lucky, that was all they'd ask of her. She got up and made her way over to Captain Coraleone. The keel was nothing more than a piece of wood glued to the bottom of the boat with a strip of flywood raveled in along its length. She recognized the rare wood at once from its dull ebony cast. These people weren't just regular bandits. Fisty's gang must be wealthy.

"What if you cut the remaining keel down into sections and reposition them along the bottom of the boat?"

"On a calm day, that would work," Captain Coraleone agreed. "Trouble is, the Great Lake's full of waves. Without the full measure of flywood to keep us aloft, they'll swamp us in no time." Lizzie bared her shark's teeth in a derisive smirk. Ermin ignored her. If Lizzie had any better ideas, why didn't she offer them? "What we really need is more lift," the Captain explained. "Failing that, we'll have to paddle."

Not if they could fly above the waves instead. The beginnings of a bargain sparked in Ermin's mind. The Speedwell's could provide speed, but Ermin didn't have any tools. Captain Coraleone had plenty of tools but no Speedwell's. With tools, Ermin could restart her business and earn favors—favors that would keep them safe all winter. "I'll trade you," she told Captain Coraleone. "Your tools in exchange for an airborne canoe."

"What are you going to do, stick the canoe on your back and swim?" Lizzie sneered. "The lampreys will suck you dry before you're a hundred feet offshore."

"I won't need to swim." Ermin tugged the packet of Speedwell's from her sock. She felt a surge of triumph as Lizzie's mouth dropped open.

"Where did you get those?" Captain Coraleone demanded.

"It's payment from a client," said Ermin. She looked to her friends, expecting smiles and nods of approval. Instead, they stared at her, dumbfounded. All right, the Speedwell's were worth a small fortune and maybe it was foolish to show them to a gang of thieves, but didn't Georgie and Colin understand how important this bargain was? With the proper tools, they could make better shelters or barter work in exchange for room and board.

"How would you use the Speedwell's?" Captain Coraleone asked her.

"I'd split the keel, just as I said, and ravel in the Speedwell's to give the boat extra speed. You'll be driving through air, not water."

"What about waterproofing? Without it, the spray from below will only soak the threads. Then we'll be back to square one."

"Spruce gum."

"We can help with that," said Colin. Georgie, Snarl, and Mouse all nodded in agreement.

"All right, you've got yourself a deal," said Captain Coraleone. "Lizzie, get over here and help. Who knows? You might learn something."

Lizzie flashed Ermin a look of pure hatred. While Lieutenant Murthy, Myranda, and the others went off in search of spruce gum, Ermin and Captain Coraleone started sectioning the keel. As soon as Captain Coraleone's back was turned, Lizzie raked her fingernails down Ermin's arm, leaving four bloody scratches in their wake. Ermin stomped down hard on Lizzie's foot in retaliation. Hopefully, that would be the end of it. Ermin would do the work, earn her tools, and get out of here. She'd never have to see Lizzie again.

The work dragged on. Lizzie kept on giving Ermin dirty looks, but she was careful to keep her distance.

"Why don't we just use a spell?" Lizzie finally complained. "It would be a lot faster."

"How many times do I have to tell you that fixing things with magic never works?" Captain Coraleone said.

"You don't have to worry, then. You aren't very good at magic."

Ermin stared at Captain Coraleone in amazement. She'd assumed that she knew the basic spells, just like everyone else.

"That's enough out of you, my girl. There's Myranda back with the waterproofing. Go and heat it up in the fire until it spreads like warm butter, and then bring it over to me." Lizzie subsided with a glower and left. Captain Coraleone sighed. "She's right, you know. I'm not any good at magic. Never have been."

"So how did you pass... I mean, your apprenticeship... "

"Apprenticeship, nothing! Taught myself, didn't I. Magic never helped anyone fix anything, so what use was it to me? Mind you, magic wouldn't be so hard to learn if they taught us how to use it in the real world. All those blasted equations and calculations were enough to freeze my brain! Most of the people I live among are blasted fools when it comes to fixing things, so my skills have currency." Captain Coraleone gave her a shrewd once-over. "You've got a rare knack for it. How would you like to change the terms of our bargain and come to work for me instead?"

"Work for you?" Ermin echoed foolishly.

"No, for the Queen. Pay attention, girl! I'm offering you a full apprenticeship in exchange for your threads."

A full apprenticeship! It's what Ermin had always wanted.

She was so shocked, she hardly knew what to say. "What about my friends?"

"Loyalty—I like that. Your friends can come along if they like. We'll find a use for them, never fear." An apprenticeship for herself and a place for everyone else besides. It seemed too good to be true. Every bone in Ermin's body shouted yes. *Yes!* But she could only answer for herself. "I have to ask them."

"Why don't you talk it over and give me your answer in the morning? The gum will take at least that long to cure."

"All right." All thoughts of Lizzie dissolved in a fizz of euphoria.

"An apprenticeship sounds fine for you, but what about the rest of us?" Georgie demanded when Ermin told them about the offer. "I don't fancy indenturing myself to anyone for the next seven years. Especially not to someone I don't even know."

Snarl placed a protective arm around Mouse's shoulders. "I'm not handing Mouse over to anyone."

"You could still see him," Ermin argued. "You'd both be indentured to the same person."

"How do you know? I didn't escape Rory only to become a slave to somebody else. I've heard enough. Come on, Mouse." Snarl and Mouse headed off toward the shelter.

"Are you happy?" Georgie asked. "I thought you really liked Mouse. How can you agree to letting someone enslave him?"

Ermin lowered her voice. "How is it any different from joining the Resistance? You think the wizards won't press us into service? We can't join them anyway, not unless you and Colin are willing to reveal yourselves to Snarl and Mouse. I don't want to be yoked to a bunch of wizards who know nothing about fixing and will only look down on me for not being able to do magic." She took a deep breath. It was time to tell Colin and Georgie the truth. "I don't want to join the Resistance. I'll have no work of my own and no way to learn anything."

"It'll be the same for us if we join Captain Coraleone's gang. I want to fight alongside the wizards, and I can't do that if I'm indentured to a mechanic! Look, if you want to sign the ledger, go ahead. I won't stop you. I'm going to join the Resistance. And another thing—if you sign on with the Captain, we'll be keeping the carpet."

"I'm the one who fixed it. With my own Speedwell's too."

"It doesn't matter. As soon as you sign the ledger, the Captain will own you and all your belongings—including all the Speedwell's."

"Well, I'm not handing the rest of the Speedwell's over to you either, if that's what you're suggesting."

"What about Denny Lorde?" Colin broke in.

Ermin whirled on him. "What about him?" If he cracked another joke about Denny liking her, she'd flatten him.

"You promised to pay off the debt that you owe to him."

Darn it all! She'd forgotten about her promise to Denny. She couldn't make him wait for seven years. "Maybe they'll let me repay my debt to Denny first. I'll talk to them."

"Don't be a fool!" Georgie snapped. "Once they find out that you're leaving, do you really think they're going to let you take the Speedwell's with you?"

Ermin bristled. It was one thing to feel like a fool, but quite another to hear her best friend call her that. "I'm not a fool and you're not always right. If you sign on with the Resistance, they'll take everything away from you too. Join if you like, but I'm keeping the carpet. It's mine—I fixed it. Besides, I'll need it when I go to work for Denny."

"We haven't even found the Resistance," Colin interjected before Georgie could argue. "So we don't need to decide right now. I'll go with Ermin to visit the Captain in case they try anything funny, and before you ask, no, I won't reveal myself. I'll keep to the shadows. They'll never even see me."

"Fine." Georgie turned away from them. "I'll stay here with Mouse and Snarl. Someone needs to protect them."

Wizard's pride, Ermin thought. Once Georgie got an idea into her head, she wouldn't back down. It was better if Colin came with her. It would give Georgie a chance to cool off. She'd come around to Ermin's way of thinking in the end. It was the only option that made any sense.

She and Colin set off through the woods. The air had cooled. They waded through patches of summer flowers withered to brown and black. Night birds called to one another from the shadowed arms of the trees. Just before they reached the thieves' campsite, Colin flung out a hand to stop her.

"What is it?"

"Canoe's missing."

It took Ermin a minute or two to spot the empty place where the canoe had once sat. "Maybe Captain Coraleone's taken it out on a test flight?"

"Pretty strange time for a test flight."

The back of Ermin's neck prickled with unease. Up ahead, the glow of the fire beckoned. Ermin could make out Lizzie and Myranda sitting next to it with Lieutenant Murthy. The kegs that had been stowed under the canoe now sat beside them. Ermin fixed her gaze first on Lizzie, who had a keg in her lap. Her brow creased with concentration as she funneled gray powder from the keg into a sack. When she was done, Myranda sewed up the top of the sack with a large needle. Lieutenant Murthy kept writing in a notebook she carried. As the pile of finished sacks grew, she ferried them to a new location. All was silent save for the sifting of powder and the occasional sneeze.

"What are they doing?" Colin asked.

"Nothing good."

"We should leave."

"And give away the Speedwell's I put on the canoe for nothing? They owe me for that trade! I'm getting the tools. Can you see the blanket roll?"

"Yes, it's lying on the ground right next to where the canoe used to be."

"Right—I'm getting it."

"I'll cover you."

Ermin crept around the rim of firelight to the place where they'd done the repairs on the canoe. The tools lay spread out on the blanket, exactly where Captain Coraleone had left them. Lizzie, Myranda, and Lieutenant Murthy were much too absorbed in their task to notice her presence. She carefully swaddled the tools between folds of blanket to keep them from clanking. She cradled the bundle in her arms, holding it close to her body as she crept back to Colin. Now all they had to do was to make it back to their own camp and collect the others. They couldn't stay here. Once Captain Coraleone discovered them missing, the hunt would be on. As much as she hated to admit it, Georgie was right. Captain Coraleone and her crew weren't likely to let a packet of Speedwell's slip from their grasp, not even a half-used one.

They hadn't taken more than a few paces when an explosion went off behind them. The force of it rushed through the trees and knocked them off their feet. They scrambled up and took off, not caring about the noise they were making. A blood-red conjurement leaked from Colin's fingers.

Ermin shoved his arm down. "No! We need you strong."

"Let go of me!" Colin wrenched free of her grasp. To

Ermin's amazement, the conjurement started to flow back into his fingers. She'd never seen him take power back into himself before. "Stop staring and get that carpet ready. It's time to fly."

"I can't! Not here in the trees."

"You sound just like Miss Fetchkeep. She was always telling you what you could and couldn't do, but she's not here, so stop listening to her! You can do it. The Rats' tunnels were far worse than this."

Ermin unwound the carpet from her shoulders and shoved her feet into the steer straps. She didn't bother buckling herself in. There wasn't any time.

"Good to go," Colin said behind her.

She slapped her palm down on the activator and leaned forward. The carpet sprang to life. There was no chance to worry. Her mind and body were kept busy as she swerved around stumps, rocks, and clusters of saplings. She didn't like to think of what her driving would have been like without having navigated the Rats' narrow tunnels.

"The field's just up ahead," said Colin. "I can smell it."

Ermin could only smell smoke, but she trusted Colin's wizard instincts. She put on a fresh burst of speed, aiming for a gap in the trees. Twigs clawed at her face but she kept going, spurred on by the thought of any pursuers chasing after them. They broke through the trees. Ermin cupped her hands around her dry mouth, trying to summon the cray call, but there was no need. A scruffy figure sprang up from the low-lying scrub and charged, her too-big boots smacking against her heels. Georgie fell face first onto the carpet.

"Where are Mouse and Snarl?" Ermin asked.

"Already gone."

"Shh!" Colin held a finger to his lips. "Listen."

The carpet hovered over a sea of silver grass. Its fringed

edges hardly rippled, as if they, too, sensed something in the stillness.

"I don't hear anything," said Ermin.

"That's what's so strange. And look." Colin pointed toward the treeline. "No fire."

Ermin twisted around. It was true. No hungry flames licked at the trees. No plumes of smoke rose into the sky. There was no trace of the explosion anywhere.

Chapter Ten

Ermin surveyed the row of trading shacks before her for signs of intruders. It had become a habit during the past couple of weeks. The beach was deserted. The last of the traders had sailed away in October, not wanting to risk their ships in the winter gales, and the merchants had long since abandoned the shacks for their warm shops. The shacks lay far enough to the west of Garrison Creek to remain an unattractive option to other orphans. Without the carpet, Ermin would have rejected them too. She'd carefully examined all of the cabins and had chosen the sturdiest for their winter home. The roof and floor were sound, but seasons of rough weather had pried some of the mud and straw away, leaving gaps between the boards. Colin and Georgie had promised to fill in the cracks, but they'd only caulked a small section before abandoning the project.

It was maddening, the way they kept putting off the work! They flew around on the carpet all day, searching for the Resistance, until Ermin was driven to complete the job herself. Was she the only one who understood how important it was to prepare for the winter? It sure felt like it.

Rain hissed in the grass. A strong gust of wind blew over the lake, driving the clouds before it like a flock of gray-bellied sheep. A sun lamp from a distant field provided a flare of gold—the only light on an otherwise dreary day. Ermin pulled an almost-new piece of oilcloth over her head in an effort to keep herself dry in the misting drizzle. She'd bargained for it by fixing a calculating abacus for a grocer's assistant. She'd also fixed his wooden leg brace for a sack of cabbages, potatoes, and carrots—good ones, with no bruises or worm holes.

"You don't have to do that," a voice behind her said. Ermin whirled. Georgie stood there, a frown knitting her brow. "Not when we've already said we would finish."

Finish? They'd hardly even started! "When will that be?"

"When we've finished searching, of course! I think we can squeeze in one more run, now that the rain's let up."

"Rain that's bound to turn into snow any day now. Winter won't wait."

"I know, I know." Georgie held up both her hands. "And we will finish, I promise. You know how important it is for us to find the Resistance. We're bound to connect with them soon. I'm sure of it."

"The only thing I'm sure of is that we've got a lot of work ahead of us, and so far I'm the only one doing any of it."

"We might not need to do that work at all if we find the Resistance."

"Only you've been searching every day for weeks and you still haven't found them."

"It's only two weeks, and they're hard to find. You know that."

"I also know that those cabin walls aren't going to caulk

themselves. I think we should drop the search until spring at least. We've got more than enough work to do as it is."

"So you don't want us to find the Resistance, is that it?" Georgie's voice was tight.

"I want us to survive the winter! That depends on all of us working together as a team to fix up the shack. We need to gather as much food and fuel as we can before we're snowed in. Not flying about all day looking for wizards that don't want to be found."

Georgie waved her hand in a dismissive gesture. "A thousand things could happen to us out here. That's why I want to find the Resistance: so we can have a real roof over our heads instead of some broken-down cabin."

Ermin bristled. She'd spent a lot of time fixing that "broken-down" cabin. Georgie, who'd done next to nothing, had no right to criticize. "Except that all of your searches have failed. Why don't you admit that you can't find them?"

"I. Will. Find. Them," Georgie said between gritted teeth.

"Thanks, but I'm putting my faith in this cabin."

"Where did you get that oilcloth?" Georgie asked unexpectedly.

"What does that have to do with anything?"

"And those potatoes? They never came from the refuse fields. They're too good. You traded for them, didn't you? You've been working again."

"So what if I have? We need supplies and I'm the only one who's concerned enough to get them."

"You could have told us. We've told you where we're going and what we're doing."

The accusation was so monstrous, so unfair, that Ermin hardly knew where to start. "You're hardly one to lecture me when I've done more work than the two of you combined!"

"We're working too. Just as hard as you."

"Not around here, you're not."

They glared at each other. Butting heads with Georgie was nothing new, but the stakes were now so high, neither one of them dared to walk away like they usually would. A two-noted whistle from Colin broke the standoff. He'd obviously taught Georgie their secret signal.

Georgie stomped off down the beach and disappeared behind the row of cabins. A short while later, the carpet flew out over the lake with Georgie at the helm. All that flying around for days and nothing to show for it, despite the fact that they both were wizards. What a waste of time!

Ermin wouldn't have noticed the carpet shift direction if she'd turned her attention back to the job at hand. Instead, she stood there fuming, watching them fly away. Georgie didn't fly east toward town. She made a reverse arc around the lake and headed back toward the beach. The only building that lay this far west was the old abandoned brickworks. Did they really think the Resistance was hiding out in there?

Georgie flew straight into the ruins. Ermin shaded her eyes, expecting to see the carpet skimming across the sand on the other side, but it never reappeared. What were they doing? Not searching for the Resistance, that much was certain. Ermin straightened with a grim determination. She'd go to the brickworks and find out the truth for herself.

She checked the fastenings on the blanket roll tool holder, then hauled it onto her back. It was far too valuable to leave behind. The bundle no longer seemed as heavy as it had a week ago. Maybe she was getting stronger from all the work she was doing.

She set off down the beach. A thick sludge oozed beneath her feet, runoff from the surrounding wetlands. As angry as she was, she chose her steps carefully, seeking out rocks and stones or tufted hillocks in order to prevent herself from slipping into a quagmire. It was the first time in weeks she'd let herself stop work to go for a walk. With every stride, the tension in her mind and body loosened and the world grew more expansive. Time had narrowed around her, confining her to an ever-urgent present where only the most immediate necessities mattered: staying safe, keeping warm, finding food. Meanwhile, the future—her future—slipped past unnoticed, lost inside a string of work-filled days. And for what? She was no closer to getting an apprenticeship than Colin and Georgie were to finding the Resistance. If they trusted her so little that they had to lie to her, then why was she working so hard to keep them together? With her new tools, and if she could get the necklace and accounts book from the school, maybe the time had come for her to strike out on her own and let Colin and Georgie deal with the drafty cabin!

It took her nearly half an hour to walk to the brickworks. Out of breath and clammy with sweat, Ermin heaved herself onto the cracked stone platform that had once been a floor. Most of the walls around her had collapsed except for a chimney that pointed a red-bricked finger at the sky. Smoke curled up from its tip. Colin and Georgie must have lit a fire. Ermin followed an arched passage that led through the rubble, picking burrs from her clothes as she went. The passage emptied into a courtyard with the chimney on her left, its base buried by a mound of fallen bricks. She'd have to climb up that mound in order to see what Colin and Georgie were up to. She was tempted to charge straight in and confront them, but what would be the point of that? They'd lied to her once. What would stop them from lying again? She'd learn far more by stealth. Slowly, she picked her way up the mound and peered over the edge.

Colin and Georgie stood before the old kiln. Its doors were

missing. A red-orange glow washed over their faces, making them look more like wizards than ever. The carpet lay abandoned on the mildewed paving stones behind them. As Ermin watched, Colin reached into the coals and pulled out two roast potatoes that he'd obviously filched from their stash. He must have used a conjurement because his hand went through the flames completely unscathed. Ermin noticed that Colin ate using his left hand. A black and brown wing tip protruded from the end of his right sleeve.

"We can't keep this up for much longer," he said.

"We can't stop, not until we get it right."

Colin shook out his wing in agitation. "I'm beginning to wonder if I'll ever get it right."

"You'll have to try harder or we'll always be dependent on the carpet," said Georgie. "I'll go again. Watch me."

Georgie raised her arms. A purple haze stole over her body. Her neck lengthened then narrowed to the diameter of a thick pipe. Her head shrank to the size of a knob, her pursed lips stretching out to form a triangle of purplish horn. Georgie's arms flattened and spread out, like batter being poured onto a hot griddle. Her fingers fused together into flippers that narrowed to a long point. A few feathers popped out, only one or two at first, followed by a flurry that broke out all over her body. When the haze cleared, a wild goose stood in Georgie's place, its neck bending in a graceful S shape. It fixed two black, beady eyes on Colin and flapped its wings.

Ermin clapped both hands to her mouth to stop herself from crying out.

Colin flung up his wing. Mist trailed down from its tip and enveloped him in a red haze. He gave an anguished cry as his skin cracked open, exposing brown and white feathers underneath. With a horrible, squelching sound, he turned himself inside out. A black goose neck and head with white markings burst forth like a striking snake between his two spread wings. It was like watching a nightmare come to life. Ermin was afraid she might be sick. Colin's human legs, still clad in St. Anselm's coveralls, remained unchanged. He let out a despairing honk.

The other goose hissed and lunged, giving his leg a sharp nip. Colin beat his wings. Red mist seeped down from the tips to cover his legs, which shrank to two black sticks ending in webbed paddles. Together, the two geese waddled unsteadily across the floor.

Ermin ducked out of sight. Horror and anger surged through her with equal force. If she'd been a wizard, she'd have fired her own conjurement at the two geese, but she wasn't a wizard. She was just an ordinary, unmagical girl who'd been stupid enough to believe the lies of her friends. Colin and Georgie weren't searching for the Resistance. They were too busy practicing transformations. But why go to all the trouble of hiding it?

A sick realization crashed over her. They were angry about losing Snarl and Mouse, so angry that they'd planned to transform themselves into geese and fly away. No wonder they weren't keen to do any work! Why bother, when they'd already planned to leave?

How many times had they come here to the brickworks when they'd claimed they were out on a search? How many times had they insisted on using the carpet, only to carelessly abandon it on the damp floor? They could have easily walked to the brickworks but had used the carpet to cover up their lie. Well, Ermin would have it back, and there was nothing they could say or do to stop her.

Honks echoed through the brickworks. Two geese soared upward. It was probably just a test flight to see if Colin could hold his shape. If so, she didn't have much time.

She slithered down the brick mound, not caring how much

noise she made. The carpet was damp but not soaked. It should still fly. She pushed the activator, insanely relieved when it powered up. She parked the carpet in a hover, jammed her feet into the steer straps, then thrust her whole body forward. The sudden whoosh of air sucked the breath from her lungs as she soared free of the brickworks. She dropped into a rider's crouch, urging the carpet on. Strands of hair whipped loose and slapped against her face. She hardly noticed. She was fused to a single purpose: to retrieve her accounts book and Miss Fetchkeep's necklace from her workshop. But before she could do either, she had a call to make.

Ermin made several passes with the carpet before she felt brave enough to set down on a flat roof that overlooked John Smith's forge. She scanned the neighboring rooftops for any sign of Rats but saw only a jumble of chimney pots. She restrained her impulse to fly straight down into the yard. Rats could be hiding down there and she'd never know it. She wasn't about to give Rory one more reason to chase her.

All this thinking about the Rats stirred a distant memory of Snarl and Mouse sitting together on a barrel. A sudden pang of regret hit her. Maybe if she hadn't pushed so hard for the apprenticeship, they'd still be around. Maybe not. They'd never taken any pledge or sworn any oaths to each other. Ermin was just glad they'd escaped. Of course, that gave Rory yet another reason to hunt her down: to exact revenge on her for stealing two of his Rats. Would the settling of scores never end?

Speaking of scores, she had one of her own to settle. She pulled the carpet tight around her shoulders and shimmied down the nearest drainpipe. No Rats, as far as she could see. That was one thing that had gone right today. The forge was quiet, the fires cold. Was John Smith sleeping off one of his drunken rages or had he gone to the pub, leaving behind a trail of broken chairs and bruised limbs? If it was the former, Denny had likely fled the shop, but if it was the latter…

Forgetting caution, she ran into the yard. As she raced past the cold furnace, a hand shot out and seized her by the wrist. A thin hand, much smaller than the heavy hand of John Smith. She was almost jerked off her feet by the sudden stop.

"What are you doing here?" Denny hissed. He'd been crouched down before a mangled mess of parts and gears, but he rose to his feet.

"Come to pay off my debt, haven't I."

"Well, it's taken you long enough—so long that I thought you'd run off."

"I already told you that I can't pick up my messages. I'm sorry it's taken me so long to get back to you. I had to leave town in a hurry." Ermin hoped that Denny would believe her. She'd told him as much of the truth as she dared to admit, and he'd never been one for prying.

"Oh." The scowl on Denny's face softened. Ermin noticed the fresh purple bruise on his cheek.

She bit her lip. There was no point in asking questions. Everyone in the Creek knew that Denny was indentured to a drunken brute. What would be the point of drawing attention to something he couldn't fix or change? "I came by to ask if there's anything that needs fixing."

"The mechanical bellows are broken. John Smith took a pry bar to them. I saved some of the pieces, as you can see."

Ermin suppressed a sigh. Reconstructing mechanical bellows that had been smashed to pieces was a lot of work, none of it easy. Denny was going to get his money's worth, and no mistake. "John Smith's out?"

"He's not here. I'd have warned you away if he was." A faint smile twitched at the corners of Denny's lips.

Ermin put her hands on her hips. "Denny Lorde, is there something you're not telling me?"

A smile broke clear across Denny's face. "He's gone to prison! The bellows weren't the only thing he went after with his pry bar. He laid out the two Magistrates who came to investigate the ruckus." Denny's expression sobered. "One of them wasn't much older than me. He's still in hospital." He led Ermin to a workbench where a number of broken widgets and gears were laid out along the top edge. "I've been putting the whole pieces over here."

She nodded her approval. "Good. I'll see what I can do to make new parts out of the broken ones." Who knows? She might be able to do a functional rebuild in a week or so. Not that it would be easy, but at least with her new tools she had a chance of doing the job. She unrolled her tool kit.

Denny let out a low whistle. "You've come up in the world! Where did you crib all of that swank?"

"Traded for it, didn't I."

"What did you do, spin copper wire into gold?"

Just about, she thought.

"Why don't you take off your cloak?"

"Can't. It's my lucky charm." Ermin drew the carpet tighter around her shoulders. It was a good thing she'd thought to wear it underside up to conceal the activator button. If Denny was dazzled by her tools, there was no telling what he might think— or do—if he learned about the flying carpet. She needed him to be on her side, which meant telling him as little as possible.

"How fast can you work?" Denny asked her.

"If all goes well, I can make the bellows functional in about a week. A full rebuild will take longer. It depends on how quickly we can get the materials."

"Make me a list." Denny pulled a notebook out from under the workbench. "I'll go around to the shops first thing in the morning."

"What's the rush? After what John Smith did, he'll be lucky to get out before the spring." People had been sent to the Scrawlings for far less.

Denny's fingers drummed on the workbench. He seemed much twitchier than usual. *No, not twitchy—excited.* "I've been thinking about what will happen to me, to this place, if John Smith gets locked away. Idle forges don't get to keep their Guild licenses, do they. They get auctioned off unless there's an apprentice on the premises who can keep it running."

"So if John Smith stays locked up, the forge will be auctioned off and you'll be out on the street?" Ermin's chest tightened in anger. Hadn't Denny been through enough without losing his job and his home?

"*Unless* I can keep everything running. That's why I need you to fix the bellows, so I can fire up the forge and protect my claim."

Ermin's head spun. Was it really possible? It sounded too good to be true. "What about John Smith's family?"

"The miserable sod's got no family. Only me."

It was as if Ermin's brain had been cleaved in two: half of it occupied with mechanical details, the other half focused on Denny's astonishing news. "How did you find out that you could claim it?"

"Been reading, haven't I. Mr. Forge sometimes lets me use the Guild library—on the sly, like."

A spark of envy ignited inside Ermin. She was glad for Denny, but she could have used some time in the Guild library herself. The thought of her favorite teacher helping out someone else made her feel more alone than ever. "If you want me to get your forge up and running, you'd better leave me to my work."

"Of course." Denny straightened. "I've got to see about rounding up some extra hands. Can't run a forge all by myself."

Ermin straightened. "You'd be better off running a thorough inventory before bringing anyone else in. How many unfinished jobs does John Smith have on the books? Do you even know?"

Denny's eyes narrowed. "What do you take me for, a fool?"

"No, only a fifteen-year-old apprentice. Any new hireling will be older than you are. They'll be waiting and watching for you to slip, eager for the chance to take over the forge. And if you don't know your business, they'll be the ones who'll play you for a fool, not me."

"I'm no fool," said Denny. "I know what I'm doing, whatever you may think. What business is it of yours, anyway?"

"It's none of my business." Ermin bent to her work. Why *was* she worrying about Denny Lorde? The forge was his affair, not hers. She had enough troubles of her own.

Denny left. Ermin mapped out the scope of the repairs by salvaging what working parts she could from the scraps on the table. It was worse than she'd thought. This job would tie her up for weeks if she let it, and it would be expensive. Nothing she could do about that. She'd just started to scribble down the list of materials Denny had asked her for when he returned.

"You work fast," he said with grudging admiration.

"Maybe so." Ermin shrugged off the compliment. "There's one more thing. Our agreement was only meant to cover the occasional repair, not a job that ties me up for weeks on end. If you want me to do more than a patch job, we need to come to a new arrangement."

"What do you have in mind?"

"A complete rebuild for the full price of my debt."

"I'll only have use of your services for two weeks."

"The way I see it, you need the bellows to claim your prize. I doubt you'll rest easy, trusting your future to a patch job."

Denny heaved a sigh. "Fine. You've got me—this time." He took out the notebook and patted his pockets for a pencil. "Oh, I almost forgot." He drew a newspaper clipping out of his pocket and unfolded it. "Did you see this?"

Ermin took the clipping from him. "What is it?"

"It's the reply to that ad you ran in the *Sentinel*. I cut it out for you, just in case you missed it."

Ermin had forgotten all about the ad. The day she'd come here with Colin and Georgie seemed like a lifetime ago. She squinted down at the small print, smudged from being kept in Denny's pocket for so long.

Baker's dozen wanted for party. Balanced scales only.

At first glance, the message was clear enough: the writer wanted to buy thirteen unspecified baked goods from a baker who balanced their scales to zero before weighing up the price. Only there was no date, and a baker's dozen of anything wasn't enough to supply a whole party. The message reminded Ermin of the word problems she'd wrestled with on her exams. She crumpled the note in disgust and shoved it into her pocket.

"Bad news?"

"Not exactly. Listen, do you know of anyone who'd be willing to trade room and board for the winter?"

Denny flashed her a broad smile. "Sure! I'll trade you room and board in exchange for helping me get the forge up and running."

"What, me stay here?"

"Why not? There's plenty of room."

Ermin thought about it. Fact was, she trusted Denny.

Wintering here at the forge would surely be better than shivering alone for months inside a drafty cabin. The forge would be warmer, drier, safer. Closer to jobs too. "What do you have in mind?"

"Just some routine maintenance... and maybe some double-checking of the books and inventory." It was as close as Denny would ever come to an apology.

"Done."

They shook hands and spat on the ground. Denny didn't even complain about her greasy hands. She wiped them off on a clean rag.

"I've got to pick up a few things. I'll be back."

"I'll be here." Denny walked her to the courtyard.

Outside, a rare clear night awaited. Stars spilled onto the fabric of the night sky, like tiny buttons surrounding a sickle moon.

"Pretty, isn't it?" Denny said. "Look, you can see Aquarius, the water bearer, and Pegasus, the winged horse."

He pointed to a cluster of constellations, his finger tracing invisible patterns among the stars. No matter how much Ermin tried to follow the lines, she could see nothing remotely resembling a human figure, let alone a winged horse.

"Libra's my favorite, but you can only see her from April to July. I used to imagine her up there in the sky weighing John Smith's evil deeds, which were so bad that they broke her scales."

"Or maybe this Libra of yours is the one who tossed him in jail." Ermin hefted her tools. "I'll see you tomorrow."

"Tomorrow."

Denny stood in the yard watching her go. It was far too dangerous for Ermin to take off in front of him. She was forced to make her way down the street on foot. The shops on either side were closed and cloaked in shadow. After a quick glance back over her shoulder to make sure that Denny could no longer see her, she shimmied up a drainpipe, peeking over the edge to check for any sign of Rats. All clear. From her new vantage point, she could see Garrison Creek spread out before her. No wonder the Rats had taken to the rooftops. Tracking marks would be easy up here.

Denny still stood in the yard under the swirl of stars. As Ermin watched, he rubbed the back of his neck, kicked a stone into the street. She didn't dare take off, not when there was a chance that he might see her. She settled down to wait. Denny jammed both hands into the pockets of his leather apron and began to pace the yard. Up and down, up and down. If she were Libra, she'd have thrown her scales right at his head to drive him inside. After walking up and down for a long while, Denny finally let himself into the house. Rusty hinges squeaked as the door opened and shut, and the latch bar dropped into place with a wooden clunk. Ermin almost cheered. She jumped onto the carpet and slipped off the edge of the roof, careful to ride low until she reached the end of the street. As she jumped to lift, her feet slipped on the slick wool. She'd forgotten to fasten her steer straps.

"Slow down, girl," she muttered to herself as she buckled up the straps.

Colin and Georgie must have returned to the cabin by now. She could imagine Georgie flying off in a snit, but Colin wouldn't leave without telling her. Not the Colin she knew. Mind you, that Colin wouldn't have kept secrets from her either. Memories of all the solo work she'd done while Colin and Georgie skipped off together wound around her stomach in a miserable knot. She'd almost rather have endured one of Rory's beatings. It would have hurt less.

She shook herself. It didn't have to hurt at all. Let Colin and Georgie cover their skins in goose feathers. Why should she care? She'd made a bargain with Denny that would see her through the winter. She'd be free of lying wizards and their conjurements forever. One more trip, and she'd be launched into her new life. In the distance gleamed the bald dome of the St. Anselm's cupola. Ermin turned her carpet toward it.

Chapter Eleven

St. Anselm's looked the same as it always had, a solid brick fortress in the middle of a shadowy world. Ermin flew over the back fence, the carpet skimming low enough to touch the tops of the weeds and grasses. She drew up beside the Old Chapel and parked behind a strand of winter hydrangea. With any luck, the snowy flowers, some as big as cabbages, would hide the carpet from view. A cold wind rippled through the fields. Ermin shivered. Soon not even the flyers she'd lined her smock with would be enough to keep the cold at bay.

Crickets chirped in the inner recesses of the building. The ceiling had sprouted a dozen new leaks. Ermin rushed past the fallen tapestry and down the damp stone steps to the workshop. The first thing she saw was her old tool belt sitting atop her workbench. Essey had returned it, just as she'd said she would.

The necklace and the accounts book were exactly where Ermin had left them. She wrapped the book up in a piece of oilcloth and tucked it into the front bib pocket of her coveralls along with the necklace. She tucked the portable glim boxes into her other pockets. They were too good to leave behind.

A dry waterfall of messages had cascaded from her workbench to the floor. Ermin bent to collect them, running through the coded names to make note of everyone she should visit. Her livelihood, such as it was, held fast. It was reassuring to know that with a bit of luck, she could trade her way to a more prosperous position. She left the messages on the floor. She'd already left the school, so she had nothing more to fear from their discovery.

Her tools were another matter. Leaving them here to be picked over was almost more than she could bear, but what choice did she have? Her blanket roll was already stuffed full. Maybe she could hide them. There were too many to fit into the space behind the brick. She glanced around the room, hoping to find a new hiding place. Horatio, standing by the door, seemed especially silent. His bony head tilted toward his own empty coffin, as if inviting her to look inside. *The coffin, of course!* It would make a perfect hiding place for the tools. She was sure its owner wouldn't mind, especially not after Horatio had invited her.

She gathered up an armful of tools and approached the coffin, then carefully arranged the tools inside and replaced the lid. When she was done, she positioned Horatio on top of the closed lid with his thin legs crossed, one on top of the other, and his hands resting neatly in his lap. The sight of death might be enough to chill the heart of any would-be thief.

"You've been a good friend, Horatio, and you've been standing here far too long. You're hereby promoted to Master of the Workshop. Guard it well."

Somehow, that made her feel better. She ran back up the stairs, past the tapestry, and out of the Old Chapel.

She was fifty feet in the air when it occurred to her that the school might yield another treasure: warm clothes. She wouldn't even need to break in. The cupola had several broken panes and hosted a flock of resident pigeons. The pigeons cocked their heads at her approach before exploding into the air with a sound like clapping hands. Inside, she skimmed across a floor slick with rain and bird droppings and came to rest in a drift of dry leaves. Beside it was the iron staircase that led down into the bowels of the school. The air inside the cupola was dank and clammy. Ermin's breath smoked in front of her as she tiptoed toward a collection of old steamer trunks. They were protected by a thick layer of oilcloth—another treasure. She tore the oilcloth away from the trunks, then folded it to fit the carpet, securing the ends under the steer and passenger straps. The fit wasn't perfect, but with any luck she'd covered up enough of the carpet so it wouldn't get wet.

Each trunk held a collection of used clothes in different sizes to fit the many orphans. She and Colin had often been brought up here to mend the clothes during their detentions. A cold fist of memory squeezed her heart. *Don't think about him,* Ermin told herself as her fingers unlatched the cold metal clasps on two trunks: one for indoor clothes and one for outdoors.

From the indoor trunk, she pulled out bundles of smocks and coveralls, shirts, and wool socks. She stripped off her old wet clothes and dressed in layers, as she had nowhere to pack the spares. Two full changes should be enough, with a few extra shirts and pairs of socks stuffed down the front of her coveralls. She made sure to transfer the necklace and her accounts book into the bib of her new coveralls. She opened the outdoor trunk. The smell of dirty linen, wet chalk, boiled cabbage, and carbolic cleanser rose to meet her. That smell had lingered like a sickness in every corridor she'd ever marched down. It had lain in wait for her underneath the sheets. It had oozed from the floors, tables, chairs, and walls. It was the smell of mothballed dreams, of hopes that had been scrubbed so many times, they'd worn clean away. Ermin had forgotten all about the St. Anselm's smell, but now it clung to her as if it would never let her go. She reached into the trunk and pulled out the first item her fingers grasped: a moth-eaten dog's-wool cloak in black and brown plaid. It would have to do. She slammed down the lid, trapping the air with its memories inside. She wrapped the cloak around her shoulders. Ugly as it was, the fabric had been boiled down to a felt so dense, the rain would have a hard time penetrating despite its many holes.

Behind her, the spiral staircase creaked, as if someone had placed a foot down on one of the steps. "Is anybody up there?" a low, croaking voice called out. Ermin froze. It was Miss Fetchkeep. "Ermin, is that you?"

A chill crawled up Ermin's back. How could Miss Fetchkeep possibly know that she was up here?

"I don't blame you for running away," Miss Fetchkeep said. "I imagine the exam results were too much for you. To try so hard and to fail so badly... for the third time too. Such a pity!"

Shame boiled up in Ermin. She closed her eyes tightly and didn't reply.

"Did Colin put you up to this? Foolish boy, throwing away his own future! Don't let him throw away yours too. Aren't you tired of eating other people's scraps, dodging Rory and his Rats? Come back to St. Anselm's! I can protect you."

The headmistress's invitation tugged at Ermin. For a moment, she was tempted. A steamy current of air blew up the staircase, a reminder of all that lay waiting for her below: a warm bed, three meals a day, solid shelter for winter, safety, an end to running. The dream shook itself out of her head, replaced by iron-cold sense. What good were Miss Fetchkeep's promises? As soon as she found out about the trading, Ermin would be out on the streets. She'd be far better off at Denny's, no matter what Miss Fetchkeep said. Ermin could never come back to St. Anselm's. Not anymore.

Another tread creaked as Miss Fetchkeep started to climb the steps. A loud metal clank reverberated around the hollow dome, catapulting Ermin into action. She raced across the slick floor and jumped onto the carpet. Footsteps pounded up the stairs behind her. She took off, ducking her head to avoid the empty window frame. There was no time to fasten the steer straps, gripped as she was by an almost uncontrollable desire to remain hidden. She aimed for Lake Street, where carpet cabs paraded up and down, swaying slightly under the weight of passengers gathered together under protective awnings. Fast and reckless Ermin flew, in a haze of panic as she merged with the busy street below. She threw the hood of the cape over her head, hoping to blend in with the other cloaked and hooded drivers. She cast a quick glance back over her shoulder. The cupola was lit up from the inside, like a crystal skull. The headmistress stood before the empty frame Ermin had flown through seconds earlier, holding a lantern aloft. Ermin couldn't shake the feeling that Miss Fetchkeep had seen through her disguise in the same mysterious way she'd known that Ermin had broken into the cupola. Even now, her sharp eyes were hunting for Ermin among all the other Lake Street drivers. As she weaved in and out of traffic, she felt the headmistress's eyes lock onto her, like a hawk sighting a sparrow.

Ermin flew straight back to the cabin. She told herself that she was glad to find it cold and dark. She was still too rattled to face another confrontation. She didn't know what she would have said to Colin and Georgie if they'd been here, anyway. Nothing that would have changed their minds. Or hers.

She knew she should grab whatever supplies she could and go. Instead, she tilted her head back, trying to find the constellations Denny had pointed out to her. The stars all looked the same: cold and uncaring. She let her eyes drop. That's when she saw it: the lurid green glow that pulsed from the brickworks.

A tracking fog.

The wizard hunters had come calling.

Ermin ran to the carpet and slammed her fist down hard on the activator. As the carpet shot forward, the wind screamed a warning in her ears. *Magistrates.* That's who she'd be up against. Unmagical Ermin with no innate wizardry and not even a bewitcher to her name. Not that it would have done her much good. She'd have to rely on the elements of stealth and surprise, her flying skills, and a very, very fast carpet. Once she had Colin and Georgie, she'd fly so fast that no Magistrate would catch them. Only how would she rid Colin and Georgie of the clinging grip of the fog? She told herself not to worry. She was getting too far ahead of herself. The first step was to find out exactly what she was up against: how many hunters were in the patrol and what weapons they had.

She landed in the brush and approached from the back where it was darkest, towing the carpet by its mooring rope. The arched passage yawned in front of her, a green glow faintly visible at the far end. A quick check confirmed that no guards had been posted. Just one hunter, then. She emerged into the courtyard. Discarded potatoes rolled across the stone floor like giant marbles. Ermin stowed them away in her cloak. If Colin and Georgie were caught in the grip of blowback, even raw potatoes would help. Green light flickered on the other side of the mound. The hunter had holed up near the chimney.

Slowly, slowly, she picked her way up the mound. At first, she couldn't see anyone. Not Georgie or Colin, or even the hunter. The flames from the fire had died away and the tracking fog threw only a muted light over the scene. She'd have to get closer. She slid down the mound, wincing as bricks clattered onto the pavement below. As soon as her feet hit the ground, she ran to the great kiln and crouched down. Nobody came. As her eyes readjusted to the murky light, a boot came into view, a shred of ragged newspaper sticking out of its sole. Ermin crawled a little farther and swallowed a gasp of horror as the entire scene revealed itself.

Mr. D'Arcy blocked her way. He lay slumped on the floor between Colin and Georgie, legs splayed out in front of him like a rag doll's. Colin had been chained to one of the kiln doors by his wrists. Georgie was lying unconscious on the floor—or worse. The top of D'Arcy's bald head shone green from the pulsating glow of the tracking fog. Both Colin and Georgie were coated in it. Not good. Ermin's eyes fell on the bewitcher that sat on the floor. At least that's what it looked like: a square black box, perhaps a bit smaller than most of the bewitchers she'd seen. A narrow wire snaked out from the machine, ending in a padded bracelet that was strapped to D'Arcy's wrist. A second wire and bracelet were attached to Georgie.

Ermin gingerly eased the rolled blanket from her shoulder, wincing at the clanks made by the tools shifting around inside. She unrolled it, keeping her eyes fixed on D'Arcy. He didn't move. It almost seemed as if he'd been knocked out. She saw no sign of burned-out flares, which was strange. Hunters usually signaled their captures, but D'Arcy hadn't lit any flares.

Armed with some sharp cutters and a pair of pliers, Ermin rerolled the blanket and slung it over her shoulder, stepping gingerly over D'Arcy. She picked up a brick as an afterthought.

She kept her eyes on D'Arcy, ready to hit him as soon as he stirred.

"Ermin."

Ermin nearly jumped out of her skin. She was about to throw the brick but stopped when she saw Colin staring at her, his eyes wide. D'Arcy was still out cold. Quickly, she cut Colin free and helped him onto the carpet. She was about to return for Georgie, but he put out a hand to stop her. "No, she's in too deep. You might hurt her."

"What do you mean?"

Colin motioned feebly toward the courtyard. She towed him out of the kiln room and up the mound of bricks.

"The machine—it's... doing something to her."

"What?"

"I don't know."

Ermin's skin crawled. "Wait here."

"No!" Colin grabbed hold of her sleeve. His grip was surprisingly strong. He must have partially regenerated. "You don't know what you're up against. D'Arcy's...changed." His voice dropped to a whisper.

"Changed, how?"

"When we were fighting, he cast spells without even using a bewitcher. The spells left a trail of brown smoke, like conjurements."

"So he's a wizard."

"Maybe. I don't know. He's doing something terrible to Georgie. The machine is making her sick."

Ermin had heard enough. "Come on."

Together, they clambered down the mound of bricks into the kiln room. "We're going to tow the carpet over to Georgie," said Ermin. "After I cut her free, we've got to load her onto the carpet as fast as we can."

"No, you can't! What if you hurt her?"

Ermin whirled on Colin. Every bit of her forgotten anger rose to the surface. He'd been planning on leaving her behind without a word. Now he wanted to waste time arguing with her? "We don't have a choice! Not unless you want to take D'Arcy with us. No? Then you'd better start hauling as soon as I make the cut."

Ermin crept forward with her cutters in one hand and a brick in the other. Colin followed, towing the carpet and carrying a brick of his own. He parked the carpet beside Georgie and grabbed her by the armpits. D'Arcy didn't move. Ermin had walked past enough opium dens to know what the slack-jawed stupor of an addict looked like. D'Arcy looked exactly like the denizens of those dimly lit rooms. The small metal box clicked and whirred. Whatever it was doing to Georgie, it looked like it was doing the same thing to him.

She brandished her cutters. Georgie's bracelet fell away on the second snip. Purple sparks sprayed in all directions, landing on Georgie's prone form. D'Arcy's head jerked upright. His face had turned a deep wine color. Even the whites of his eyes had turned purple. He looked every bit the monster that he was. Ermin grabbed Georgie's ankles. Together, she and Colin tossed Georgie onto the carpet.

"Stop!" D'Arcy roared.

Ermin hefted a heavy brick and hurled it at his head. D'Arcy blocked it as easily as if he were batting a thrown pillow aside, but he wasn't prepared for the pile of bricks Colin dumped on him. He fell to the ground, buried in rubble.

"Ermin, come on!" Colin shouted.

Ermin hesitated. The machine was still sparking, still attached to D'Arcy's ankle. She was vaguely aware of Colin buckling Georgie into a pair of passenger's straps but remained focused on the machine. However it functioned, whatever its purpose, it seemed like something D'Arcy shouldn't have.

"Ermin!"

She ran, not to the carpet, but to D'Arcy. She brandished her cutter and snipped right through the wire then seized hold of the machine. The carpet was by her side in an instant. Ermin jumped on and jammed her feet into the second pair of passenger straps, interlacing her arm with Georgie's.

D'Arcy clawed free of the brick pile, his piano-key teeth bared in a snarl. Coffee-colored sparks dropped from his fingers. "Give me back my transpositor!"

Colin jumped so high, his feet strained against the steer straps. The carpet sprang into the air with a jolt. Ermin toppled sideways, landing on top of Georgie. It seemed like a good place to stay. A smoking brown missile shot past her head, blasting a hole clean through the wall.

"Hold on!" Colin dropped into a rider's crouch and aimed for the archway.

Ermin closed her eyes. She couldn't look. A few seconds later, cool, damp air brushed her cheek, telling her they'd made it through. D'Arcy's detonations exploded on the walls and floor behind them. There was no doubt about it. He was now casting spells without a bewitcher. She opened her eyes and looked back. D'Arcy was running—no, leaping—along the passageway. With each step he took, he covered about twenty feet—or more.

"He's charmed his feet," Ermin shouted. "Fly out over the lake."

She wrapped her arms more tightly around Georgie. She'd never seen her so still. At least they'd freed her from D'Arcy's clutches. She glanced back over her shoulder again. A black shape churned through the water, like a shark trailing a ship.

"He's still following us," said Ermin.

"What should we do?"

There was only one place Ermin could think of that might be safe. "Head for Denny's."

Colin flew straight toward the forge without raising a single objection. Ermin didn't know how they would explain Colin and Georgie's sudden appearance to Denny. Never mind. All that mattered right now was getting to the forge before Georgie got any worse—or before the tireless D'Arcy caught up to them.

Colin landed in John Smith's yard. Although the fires were out, the cooling troughs were still full of water. Ermin threw one of Georgie's arms over her shoulder and heaved her to her feet. She and Colin were still glowing green. Traces clung to Ermin as well.

"Help me get her into the trough."

Colin wrapped Georgie's other arm around his shoulder. Together, they lowered Georgie into the water so that every inch of her was covered. It was harder heaving her out again. Colin submerged himself in the trough, swearing and sputtering. When he climbed out, Ermin sucked in a deep breath before taking the plunge herself. The water was so cold, it burned like fire. She closed her eyes and forced her head underwater. All she could hear was the sound of her own heartbeats. When she surfaced, Colin and Denny were already dragging Georgie toward the wide-open kitchen door. Ermin climbed out of the trough and staggered in after them. There was no telling where that monster, D'Arcy, had got to. And still, no flares.

Inside, Denny built up the fire. Colin propped Georgie up in a chair and wrapped her up in an old horse blanket. Ermin shivered, her thoughts as frozen and clumsy as the rest of her. She had no idea what to say to Denny, how to explain. Denny didn't say a word as he brought them dry clothes and took away their wet ones. Then he laid out bread, cheese, and ale on the table. Ermin ate and drank, her shoulders knotted with tension.

Every bang or rattle made her jump. She told herself that D'Arcy couldn't track them, not after they'd washed off all traces of magical residue. Try as she might, she couldn't relax.

She sprang up to help Colin wash the dishes and made several trips to the woodbox, piling wood they didn't need on the floor. Georgie dozed by the fire. Denny didn't say a word but followed her to the woodbox on one of her trips. He pushed his head so close to Ermin's, she felt his breath warm against her cold neck. "I'm not going to force you to share anything you don't want to, all right?"

Startled, Ermin could only nod. It was only the briefest of nods, but no doubt it meant another agreement that would increase her debt to Denny even further.

Chapter Twelve

Ermin wasn't sure how many nights she'd spent working in secret down in Denny's cellar. She'd lost track. The machine that D'Arcy called a "transpositor" had set her brain on fire.

During the day, she went through the motions of fixing the forge's bellows, but her heart wasn't in the work. Colin was sure that Georgie's illness had somehow been caused by the machine. That thought absorbed Ermin. It was all she could think about while she painstakingly reassembled the bellows or performed her share of the daily chores while a much-weakened Georgie watched from her chair. At mealtimes, Ermin barely took part in any conversation. She often stayed up late into the night, poring over the notes she had made or performing experiments on the transpositor, trying to crack its secret. Another thought had recently begun to insinuate itself into the swirling mass of questions about the machine. If she did manage to figure out how it worked, maybe she could reinvent it. After all, a machine was simply a device using power to harness forces and movement to perform an action. Change the forces and movement, and the actions the machine could perform would also be changed.

If Mr. Forge, her old mechanics teacher, thought that the Guild would be interested in her drawings, how much more interested might they be in an entirely new invention? Would it be enough to gain her entry to the apprenticeship program at the prestigious Guild Academy?

She hardly dared to admit such thoughts, even to herself. It seemed disloyal to Georgie, who lay sick upstairs. The machine had depleted her in some way. Ermin's first order of business was to figure out how it had done so and whether there was some way of reversing the action. None of this stopped her from thinking about the Academy, though: what it would be like to be admitted or to stroll through its hallowed halls, secure in the knowledge that she was being taught by the best mechanics in the settlement instead of constantly learning by trial and error.

She'd dismantled the transpositor as quickly as possible after its plunge in the water trough, laying out all the wet parts to dry. She'd had to crib some spare parts from the mechanical bellows, pretending to Denny that some of the original parts were broken. She felt bad about the lies she'd told, but she didn't want to be beholden to Denny for her room and board any longer than necessary. Up close, the box looked nothing like a bewitcher. It was missing the spell feed tray and the crank, for starters. Unlike other bewitchers, its top edge was dominated by a large yellow dial. What it did, Ermin couldn't tell. Twisting it in either direction did absolutely nothing.

Tonight, she was reassembling the transpositor for the fifth time. She could recite and fit the pieces together by heart: the electrical circuit wires, clamps and screws, six small current converters, and three long glass orbulets. The orbulets pulsed with color. Yellow, orange, and purple plumes twisted and twirled, as if fighting to escape their tubular prisons. They lay side by side in a narrow nesting box. The converters had been placed along the upper and lower edges of the nesting box and touched the tops and bottoms of the glass tubes. The converters fed straight into the wires she'd cut—the ones that had been attached to the bracelets. The machine was set up to conduct and circulate a current of some kind, but there was no plug-in or any sign of an internal energy source. Ermin sighed. How it had made Georgie sick was still a mystery. What was the connection between the transpositor and D'Arcy's conjurements? Perhaps there was no connection and D'Arcy was just a wizard hiding in plain sight, like Colin and Georgie. That would explain why he'd never sent up any flares to alert the Magistrates. Then why hunt them down in the first place?

The glim box she'd been using flickered, then started to fade. Ermin fished out her spare before it died. She was lucky that Essey had returned them, or she'd have owed Denny for dozens of burned candles. She must remember to set them out in the sun tomorrow morning to recharge. She detached the yellow orbulet and held it up to the dim light. "What are you?"

"Talking to yourself again?"

Ermin whirled to find Colin standing at the foot of the stairs. "I thought I'd find you down here."

"How's Georgie?"

"About the same. She ate some soup, though."

"That's good."

"Any luck?"

Ermin sighed. "Not much."

Colin peered down at the transpositor. "You've pulled the whole thing apart and put it back together. Again."

"And I still don't know how it works. Take this, for instance." Ermin held the yellow orbulet out at arm's length. "I have no idea what this is or what it does."

Colin took a hasty step backward. "Ugh! That yellow smoke looks almost alive."

Ermin's mind knotted around the description. The orbulet slipped from her grasp and broke in two on the floor. Yellow smoke billowed out. It coiled in on itself, bubbling and shrinking until it transformed into a small yellow flower.

"A wizard's warning!" breathed Colin.

"A what?" The flower trembled, though there was no draft.

"Wizards sometimes leave them behind to warn of danger. It's odd, though. Wizards use their own power to leave a warning."

"Maybe that's what this is," said Ermin, holding up the halves of the empty orbulet. Colin joined her, shining his own glim box down on it. The brightness instantly doubled. She could finally see without squinting.

Colin shuddered. "What was D'Arcy doing with a vial of wizard's power?"

They both stared down at the other orbulets, their orange and purple contents writhing inside. She pulled them both out and held them up to the light. Each orbulet had a tiny knob at one end. They'd been invisible before in the dim light from a single glim box. One by one, Ermin fitted them back inside the box, making sure that each knob made contact with the metal plate of each conductor.

D'Arcy's machine whirred to life with an ominous chug.

"What did you just do?" Colin asked.

Before Ermin could answer, the screwdriver she'd been using flew from her hand. It landed on top of the transpositor with a metallic clang. Ermin tried to pry it loose but the resistance was too strong, as if the screwdriver had been bolted in place. The orbulets were generating a magnetic field! Orange and purple smoke rushed through a network of glass tubes toward the top of the box, drawn in that direction by the current, erupting in orange and purple sparks from the cut wires. Ermin twisted the yellow dial. The chugging stopped. Ermin and Colin's combined breathing sounded loud in the sudden silence.

She was the first to break the silence. "That old vampire's been sucking Georgie's wizardry right out of her."

"But why?"

Ermin could almost feel the separate strands of her thoughts twisting together, making a connection. "How did D'Arcy get hold of the tracking fog? I thought it was restricted to Magistrates."

"D'Arcy was a former Magistrate, wasn't he? He still had lots of gear in his office. He must have got booted out. Why else would he work at St. Anselm's?"

"If D'Arcy's a former Magistrate, why didn't he send up any flares to alert the patrols?" She answered her own question in the next breath. "He wanted to keep all the power for himself."

Colin scratched the upper half of his right arm vigorously. A few stray feathers fell out of his sleeve.

"Molting, are you?"

Colin gaped at her. "How did... ?"

"Saw you transforming, didn't I."

"It's not what you think. I can explain."

"You told me you were looking for the Resistance, when all the time, you were working on transformations. I bet you and Georgie had a real laugh, watching me do all the work by myself. When were you going to ditch me?" The hurt came spilling out. She and Colin had been best mates since they were seven, but he'd been growing more wizardish ever since they'd left St. Anselm's. Now he'd changed into someone she hardly recognized, someone who'd discard her like the magical dunce she was.

"Ditch you?" Colin echoed. "What are you talking about? We were going to tell you the very night that D'Arcy caught us. We were practicing just to make sure that we... that I... could hold the shape. Georgie was convinced you'd try to stop us if you knew what we were doing. I never should have gone along with it, but I was so bad at transforming myself." Colin's voice lowered with shame.

He'd been a magical prodigy for years. Maybe this was the first time he'd experienced failure. "You got it in the end. You flew clear across the lake."

"You saw that? It was my first time. Georgie had almost given up on me, but I wanted to try again before we told you. I wanted to make sure that I could really do it, transform myself and hold the shape, in case we ever got separated again. It'll be so much safer when all three of us can fly."

So they weren't planning on leaving her behind after all! A wave of relief crashed over Ermin, so strong that it almost swept her off her feet. Still, that didn't excuse them from keeping secrets. "You could have said."

"I know. I'm sorry."

An awkward silence fell over them. Ermin was still angry, but at least the hurt was receding. For the first time in weeks, the metal band that had been squeezing her heart broke apart. She felt like she could breathe again. "You said that D'Arcy's conjurements left a brown residue behind."

"Like smoke, yes."

"Had you ever seen him cast like that before?"

"No, he always used a bewitcher. The residue from those is silver, not brown."

"Tell me everything you remember about being captured."

"We'd just got back from our flight," said Colin. "We should have taken a quick dunk in the lake to wash off the residue, but we were too knackered. So it must have been easy to track us. We knew something was wrong when we couldn't find the carpet; you must have already grabbed it. Not that it would have done much good. D'Arcy pounced on us like a fox and fired a couple of freeze charms at us. He put me in cuffs, then snapped on the machine. I thought it was a bewitcher until I saw what it was doing to Georgie."

"What happened to his bewitcher, anyway?"

"I never saw it; just the transpositor. The longer Georgie stayed attached to it, the worse she got. It was like she was being drained. Not like that old bag of bones. His face got redder and rounder, didn't it. And all the time, that blasted machine kept chugging away."

Ermin examined the orbulets again, their battery-like connections, the flow of the current, the colored sparks, and the small yellow flower—a warning cast by a wizard from the last vestiges of their power. Suddenly it all fell into place. That's what drove the machine: wizardry, harvested from captive wizards just like the draining platform in Redemption Square. The orbulets were a kind of battery, draining power away from wizards and transferring it to the transpositor's maker. The brown smoke from D'Arcy's conjurements proved it. For what else could have turned it brown but the mixed colors from different wizards?

"Georgie's sick because D'Arcy used the machine—the transpositor—to drain the wizardry out of her faster than she could regenerate. It's not the first time he's done it, either. The yellow and orange vials are proof of that."

Colin's eyes bugged out of his head. "Why would he do that?"

"So he could use it." Ermin stuffed a few tools into the leather apron she'd borrowed from Denny and scooped up D'Arcy's machine with both hands, cradling it close to her chest. "Come on."

"Where are we going?"

"To fix Georgie."

~

Georgie sat in the kitchen before the stove. She was wrapped up in so many blankets, it looked as if she'd woven a cocoon around herself. A whole week had passed since the attack, but she couldn't stop shivering.

Georgie's eyes darted toward Ermin as she paused awkwardly at the top of the cellar steps, then flicked away again. D'Arcy's transpositor hadn't been the only thing that had kept Ermin in the cellar. She and Georgie hadn't really spoken since their last fight. She'd been avoiding Georgie for days, but there was no avoiding her now. She took a deep breath and set the transpositor down on the table.

Georgie's eyes fastened on it. "Isn't that D'Arcy's? What are you doing with it?"

"I took it from him. Do you remember anything about that?"

A violent shiver shook Georgie's frame. "I don't want to remember."

"Georgie, she's trying to help," said Colin.

"Then why did she steal the carpet?" Georgie snapped. "We could have gotten away."

All of Ermin's anger surged forth, despite her best efforts to contain it. "Why didn't you tell me about your secret transformations?"

Georgie turned her accusing gaze on Colin. "You told her?"

"He didn't need to," said Ermin. "I saw you turn into geese for myself. I didn't buy that bunk about you and Colin finding the Resistance, so I trailed you. Good thing, too, or your power wouldn't have been the only thing D'Arcy stole."

"What are you talking about? D'Arcy didn't steal my power."

"Oh, really? Then why haven't you regenerated? Colin bounced back the day after we arrived." Ermin opened the transpositor's case to expose the orbulet filled with purple smoke. "Then there's this."

Georgie's eyes widened. "Where did you get that? It looks like... " She reached out a tentative finger, then snatched it back.

" ...wizardry?" Ermin finished. "You're right. This machine allowed D'Arcy to drain your power and turn himself into a wizard."

"I saw the old vampire doing it," said Colin.

Georgie stared at them as if they'd lost their wits. "But you can't turn yourself into a wizard! It isn't possible."

"Then how did D'Arcy cast spells without using a bewitcher? He was using your power to cast conjurements. And not just yours, either. He's drained at least two other wizards." She gestured toward the orbulets.

"One of them left a wizard's warning," added Colin.

Georgie tore her eyes away from the purple smoke of her own wizardry swirling around its narrow glass prison. "What?"

"Ermin broke one of the orbulets by accident and a danger flower sprouted on the floor. That warning must have been the last conjurement the poor wizard cast before D'Arcy... " Colin's voice trailed off.

"But that's... an abomination!" Georgie sputtered. "Redemption Square is bad enough without people running around draining wizards on their own."

"I don't think the Magistrates know," said Ermin. "D'Arcy didn't send up a single flare to signal the patrols, remember?"

"He wouldn't, would he?" said Colin. "Not if he's been secretly turning himself into a wizard. The Magistrates would drain him in Redemption Square the minute they found out."

Georgie drew her knees up to her chest, upsetting a stack of papers she'd been twisting into fuel for the stove. "What you said, about stolen power. Do you think... I mean... can it be reversed?"

"Maybe. I cut off both the cuffs, but I have an idea that maybe the transfer can be made using light." Ermin brandished the glim box.

"You mean you don't know?" Georgie's face took on a smooth, neutral blankness that Ermin had termed "St. Anselm's face." Every orphan knew how to cover their fear with a mask so as not to be seen as weak. It was a hard habit to break, even after you'd left the school.

"Well, I've never drained a wizard before or restored one to power."

Georgie flashed her a weak grin. "Fair point."

"You're lucky Ermin came before that old vampire could slurp it all up," said Colin. "The tube is only half-full."

"Well, I want it all back," said Georgie. "How long will it take? Let me guess: you don't know."

"She'll do it, however long it takes," Colin told Georgie. "Remember when she rejigged the timed lock on the pantry so we could get more food? That job took nearly a week."

Georgie laughed. "I'd almost forgotten."

Ermin grinned as she organized her tools on a cloth. The timer had been hard to crack, but going hungry had been harder—almost as hard as it was to see the energetic, irrepressible Georgie reduced to such a feeble state. It was an even greater spur to action than the hunger had been.

"Move over," Colin said to Georgie. "I'll help you twist those flyers."

He sat down beside Georgie. The two of them were so thin, they could fit together on a single chair. Remembering D'Arcy's drugged languor, Ermin detached the orange orbulet and tucked it away in her pocket. She didn't want to risk putting someone else's wizardry inside Georgie.

The old water clock in the kitchen ticked off the minutes while Ermin cut, raveled, connected, and threaded. Colin and Georgie twisted more flyers into fuel. Attaching the glim box was tricky work. The connections were fiddly and the reused wire kept breaking. Sweat dripped down Ermin's face. She reached into her pocket for a rag. A scrap of paper flew out and drifted across the floor. The newspaper clipping! She'd forgotten all about it.

Colin pounced on it at once. "What's this, a love note from Denny?"

"Don't be ridiculous! It's the answer to Georgie's ad, the one she put in the *Sentinel*. Denny cut it out for us."

"Cut it out for you, you mean." Colin blew her a string of kisses.

"What does Darling Denny's newspaper clipping say?" Georgie asked.

"Let's find out. My lovely wood raveler, how I long—" Colin stopped short. "It doesn't make any sense. Listen to this: 'Baker's dozen wanted for party. Balanced scales only.' What kind of an answer is that?"

"What kind of answer did you expect from 'Frida knits socks, two coppers a pair?'" said Ermin.

"'Frida knits socks, two coppers a pair' is the standard request for news, I'll have you know." Georgie snapped her fingers impatiently. "Give it here."

Colin handed over the clipping. Georgie frowned down at it.

"*Baker's dozen* means thirteen of something, but I don't get that bit about the scales."

"Please don't tell me I traded weeks of labor away for nothing," said Ermin.

"You traded for a message and a message is what we got," said Georgie. "All we have to do is decipher it. And before you ask, no, I don't know all the phrases. They sometimes change."

"Maybe we should go to the courtyard again," Colin suggested.

"They'll only have left the same message, not a translation."

Ermin suppressed a snort. It was a wonder the Resistance managed to communicate at all. Still, a hard-to-crack code might help to explain why they'd avoided capture for so long.

"Are you finished yet, Ermin? I'm ready for my shot."

"Give me a minute."

Although the light was only attached to the filling end and not the draining end, Ermin carved three notches into the top edge of the box, just in case. There was no point in taking any chances of the ends getting mixed up. The transpositor was dangerous enough already.

"The direction of the flow is regulated by a magnetic current generated by the wizardry itself," she told Georgie. "Since all wizardry contains electrons, the current should be more attracted to you if you've regenerated even a little."

"That's as clear as mud," said Georgie. "Go on. I'm ready."

"It might not work," Ermin warned her.

"It won't work at all if you keep on talking!"

"You're sounding more like your old self with every word," said Colin.

"Yes, indeed," Ermin said. "Essey's darling dumpling is in fine form."

"Keep it up and I'll thump the pair of you as soon as I get my juice back," said Georgie, but she was grinning.

Ermin switched on the transpositor. The machine chugged to life. She pointed the glim box at Georgie. A beam of light shot out and engulfed her. Her wiry hair slowly rose into the air until it stood out like a halo around her head. She sat taller, her bare toes gripping the floor like roots. Ermin had purposely left the back of the box exposed, so she could monitor the wizardry levels. The purple orbulet was now only a quarter full.

"How much are you going to give her?" Colin whispered.

"The whole thing." Georgie's amplified voice boomed through the kitchen.

Colin clapped his hands to his ears and backed away. Ermin would have covered her own ears if she hadn't been operating the machine. The orbulet was empty now. A few heartbeats later, the glim light blinked once, twice, before it faded. Georgie turned around to face them. Her dark brown eyes snapped and her brown skin glowed. She positively radiated energy in the cramped recesses of the kitchen.

"You look strange," said Colin. "Say something."

"I don't feel quite myself—"

Georgie's words were cut off by a honk as she suddenly shifted shape. It was nothing like the painstaking transformation Ermin had witnessed earlier. This one was a blur of shapes and colors that swirled by so fast, she couldn't pick out any specific details. Within seconds, a wild goose had materialized before them. Black and tan feathers framed its wide, snowy chest. A jet-black beak sat between piercing, intelligent eyes. This goose was regal, a queen of geese. She arched her neck and clacked her beak. Another swirl of shapes and colors, and then Georgie re-materialized. Another blur, and the goose returned, only to change back into Georgie. Georgie slipped in and out of goose shape a few more times, wrapping herself up in feathers and shrugging them off again like a cloak. It was almost dizzying to watch.

"What's happening to her?" Colin cried, as Georgie flipped back and forth between shapes.

"She must have regenerated enough on her own that returning all of the old power put her into overdrive." The extra power had nowhere to go. It was exploding out of her.

"Nonsense, I never felt better." Georgie reappeared, bent over and panting. A few stray feathers drifted to the floor. "I think I can hold my shape, but you wouldn't believe how much that goose wants out! I've heard about wizards getting lost in transition, but this is ridiculous!"

Colin was so relieved that he shoved Georgie. Georgie shoved him back. Completely overcome, Colin thumped Ermin on the back. She punched him on the shoulder. They tumbled together, laughing, their arms tangling together. Ermin wished they could stay united like this forever, just as they'd been at St. Anselm's. Why did things always have to change?

Georgie admired her reflection in a polished section of stove. "And to think that old Miss Fetchkeep put me in remedial, said I'd never amount to anything. Well, I'd sure like to show her! I bet you would too, Ermin. She was always after you about your magic."

Ermin flew to the defense of her old teacher. "It's not Miss Fetchkeep's fault I wasn't any good at it. Anyway, she gave me a workshop."

"You were good advertising for the school, and you worked for free. Or at least, that's what she thought. Anyway, what you did with the transpositor is exactly like magic. Even better."

"I bet if the Guild could see you now, you'd get an apprenticeship on the spot," said Colin.

"Too bad you're not the exam facilitator," Ermin quipped, trying to keep her voice light. In truth, she was overcome by her friends' compliments.

"About the transformations." Georgie took a deep breath. "We shouldn't have kept that a secret."

"I shouldn't have been so quick to take the carpet," said Ermin. "I thought you were going to fly away and leave me."

Georgie's eyes widened in surprise. "Why would we do that when we're all going to join the Resistance together?"

Ermin shook her head. Signing up for the Resistance made sense for Colin and Georgie; they were wizards. Ermin was an ordinary, nonmagical girl. She'd never find the mentors and teachers she needed to become a mechanic. It was as if a fissure had opened up between them, with Ermin on one side and Colin and Georgie on the other. The more Colin and Georgie pushed to join the Resistance, the more Ermin resisted, and the more the fissure widened. She was tired of feeling so fractured.

As if he could read her mind, Colin gave Georgie a poke. "Leave her alone. Help me build up the fire."

They threw a load of twisted flyers onto the glowing coals. It didn't take long for them to catch. Ermin held out her arms to the flames. She'd been so intent on her work, she hadn't noticed the cold seeping into the room.

After a while, Georgie spoke. "Do you think you can fix the other end of the transpositor—the draining end?"

"I think so. Why?"

"Because I'd like to hunt down that old skeleton, D'Arcy, and pay him back for what he did to me and all those other wizards."

"You mean go back to St. Anselm's and blast him in his own office?" asked Colin.

"That might not be as easy as you think," said Ermin. "When I broke into the cupola a week ago, Miss Fetchkeep knew who it was even without seeing me. It was uncanny, almost like she could see right through the floor."

"Does it matter?" asked Colin. "We blast D'Arcy, and then we leave. Simple. Who cares if Miss Fetchkeep knows it was us or not?"

"It matters because she'll tell the Magistrates. Then it will be our word against D'Arcy's, and he's a teacher."

"We've got all the proof we need right here." Colin tapped the transpositor.

"We can't explain how it works unless you two reveal yourselves. Then the Magistrates would take you, for sure. Plus, they'd seize the transpositor. Can you imagine what they'd do with it? We'd better steer clear of St. Anselm's. We need to find a way to discredit D'Arcy without arousing suspicion against ourselves."

All three of them fell silent. The fire shifted inside the stove, catching the corner of an unlit flyer. Ermin watched as the spreading fire made the letters glow.

Sunday, December 13, 1829
Come one, come all to the Magistrates' Ball!
7 p.m. at Frank's Hotel on Lake Street

"How strong do you think D'Arcy's connections to the Magistrates really are?" she asked Colin.

"Well, he's got a lot of gear in his office. He must know them."

"What are the odds he'll show up at the Magistrates' Ball?"

"I bet he will!" Georgie exclaimed. "Remember all those fancy clothes hanging up in his office?"

"That's all very well for him, but how will we get in?" asked Colin. "We don't have any clothes like that."

"No worries there," said Georgie. "Frank always hires extra staff to help him out. We'll get there early and stand in line—wearing masks, so we won't be recognized."

150

Colin plucked a flyer out of the fuel box. "Sunday, December 13, 1829," he read aloud. "That's tomorrow night. Will we be ready in time?"

A grim resolve hardened in Ermin. "We'll be ready, all right." She'd make sure of it, even if she had to stay up all night.

Chapter Thirteen

Ermin mouthed silent curses as she pulled open the transpositor's case for what felt like the hundredth time. She'd fitted a glim box on each end, so that draining or filling beams could be directed at a target, depending on which end was pointing up. The filling end was already marked with notches, so there was little danger of mixing them up. If only the other problems were as easy to solve!

"What's wrong with it?" Georgie asked. "You just finished testing it on me. So why isn't it working?"

"I don't know!" Ermin shone a glim box over the innards. Was she going to have to take the blasted thing apart again? She felt sick just thinking about it.

Georgie peered over her shoulder. "It's pretty rusty in there."

"Just some leftover stains," Ermin said shortly. "I cleaned up everything after the transpositor got soaked."

"Maybe I should perform a conjurement on it."

"No! Magic and mechanics don't mix. Everybody knows that."

"Denny might be back soon. We're getting down to the wire."

"The wires!" Ermin cried. "That's it! I reused the old wire. Maybe some rust has gotten into the connections." Ermin shone the glim box over the coiled circuits. "There it is." She pointed at a connection leading from the orbulets' nesting box. The segments of wire twisted around the connecting screws were so brittle, they were pulling away.

"So all you have to do is replace the wire." Georgie sounded relieved.

"Except I don't have any." Ermin pulled out the contents of her apron and her pockets—places where she was most likely to stash spare bits. Nothing. "No money to buy wire either."

Her hands flew to the front bib pocket of her coveralls before she remembered that the necklace was gone. The accounts book was there when they had arrived at Denny's, but she hadn't been able to find the necklace.

"What are you looking for?"

"Miss Fetchkeep's necklace. I could pawn it for money, as soon as the shops open."

Georgie laughed. "You nicked a necklace from Miss Fetchkeep?"

"I never nicked it! Miss Fetchkeep gave it to me."

"Miss Fetchkeep gave you a necklace?" Georgie was amazed. "Why?"

"I don't know. She said that I might like it when I got older."

"That'll be the day! Never mind. There's plenty of wire around here. All we have to do is disconnect one of the storm lamps."

"Without asking Denny?" Ermin felt guilty enough from all the lies she'd already told him without adding more.

"You can always fix it up later, with no one any the wiser. This is an emergency."

"No." Ermin pushed past Georgie and headed upstairs. She had already looked days ago, but she again searched the kitchen, then got down on her hands and knees to check to see if the necklace had rolled under the stove. She searched beneath the wooden racks they'd used to dry their clothes. They hadn't used any of the bedchambers, preferring to curl up beside the stove. The only place left to check was the yard.

Darkness was fading, the night just starting to dissolve into the pale gray clouds of morning. The air had a frosty tinge to it. A few flakes of snow drifted down from the sky. In the distance, Ermin could hear the swish of early-morning carpets and the jingle of metal tackle as farm horses pulled their carts to market. The streets would soon be stirring with sleep-tousled apprentices opening up shops and fetching water from the nearby pump. Ermin searched the entire yard but found nothing. Purple light flared at her shoulder.

"Maybe we should check the trough," said Georgie.

A skin of ice lay over the water. Georgie skimmed her glowing hands over it to illuminate the depths. Nothing. Ermin rolled up her sleeve and punched down through the ice. The shock of sudden cold made her gasp. She fished around in the trough for as long as she could stand it, then withdrew her hand. "It's not there." She dried off on a a length of rough sacking hanging from a peg in the forge. "I must have lost it at the brickworks, or else it came off when we were flying."

"We'll have to strip some wire from one of the lamps inside," said Georgie. "I'm sorry, but I don't see any other way."

"What are you two doing out here so early?"

Ermin whirled. Denny was standing in the yard. He

headed straight to the water trough and dunked his head, rubbing his hair, face, and neck. He resurfaced with a gasp and reached for the same piece of sacking that Ermin had used. He toweled off vigorously.

"Are you back from the fair already?" Georgie asked.

"I finished up my business yesterday." Denny's voice was muffled through the burlap. "I saw no point in sticking around."

Georgie got right to the point. "Do you have a spare length of wire kicking around?"

"Not offhand. Why don't you try stripping the wire from the lamp in John Smith's room? He won't be needing it any time soon."

Georgie flashed Ermin a knowing smile. "I'll do that." She hurried back inside.

Ermin's sense of relief faded as quickly as it had come. "I guess we'll have to make a new bargain." At this rate, she'd end up working for Denny permanently.

"No, we don't!" Denny's voice was sharp. "Don't you ever get tired of tallying up every little thing? I sometimes wish we could forget about keeping accounts altogether."

Ermin didn't know what to say. Bargains were currency. That was how the laws of exchange worked. What else was there?

"You'll never guess who I met at the fair," said Denny. "Miss Fetchkeep! She asked after you and sends her best."

Ermin was astonished. "Miss Fetchkeep was asking about me?"

"Yes, though why she thought I knew where you were, I can't fathom. Maybe it's because we're friends. Friends can surely spare each other a bit of old wire without asking for payment in return." Denny took a deep breath. He tilted his head back to look at the sky. "If Libra was up there balancing her scales, she'd agree with me. But it's only old Pegasus. See?"

As usual, Ermin couldn't pick out the pattern of the constellation from the few remaining scattered seeds of light. The mention of scales triggered a memory, but it faded like morning dew. The sun broke through the clouds and crested the horizon, stretching warm fingers across the yard. Ermin's shoulders, tense and hunched, slowly relaxed. The morning had never seemed so bright.

~

Frank's Hotel was a two-story stone building with two chimneys and a broad, sloping roof. Soft light shone from the mullioned glass panes that fronted the street. A wooden walkway led past the front door to a side entrance for deliveries. Beyond that was a muddy yard with a fence and a gate. A long line of urchins stretched down the walkway and down a rough path of stones that took up where the walkway ended. Ermin nudged the others forward to stand in the muck, closer to the gate. She didn't want to risk getting cut. This earned them a few nasty glares, but nobody stepped forward to challenge them. Colin had fashioned some masks for them while Ermin and Georgie had been busy fixing the transpositor. Only one other person was wearing one. The masks marked them out, but at least they wouldn't be recognized.

"If the gate doesn't open soon, they'll jump us for cutting the line," said Georgie, her voice sounding muffled through the mask. "Then we'll be too bruised and battered to get hired."

"Or too naked." Colin wore the flying carpet underneath the dog's-wool cape to keep it hidden. He fingered the cape's clasp nervously. "That fellow over there looks like he'd like to rip the clothes right off my back."

Ermin glanced over at a big boy, shivering in a too-small jacket. He shot her an unfriendly glare.

"Maybe I should disappear around the corner for a minute," said Georgie. "I could defend us better in goose shape."

"No!" Ermin fought to lower her voice. "We need you to stay in human form so you can create a diversion. We already agreed." The last thing she needed was for Colin and Georgie to start making last-minute plans—something that wizards were prone to do.

"All right, all right. It was just a thought." Georgie sounded peeved.

The plan was for Ermin and Georgie to enter the hotel and make for the gallery above the main hall, where they'd have a bird's-eye view of the guests. Once D'Arcy was spotted, Ermin would grab a tray of food from one of the servers and make her way toward him, while Georgie would create a diversion by lobbing smoke bombs into the fireplace. Ermin would turn the transpositor on D'Arcy while pretending to serve the guests. It would take the bombs several minutes to combust. Ermin and Georgie would escape under cover of the smoke, and Colin would swoop down on the carpet to pick them up.

"I think I should be the one who fires at D'Arcy," said Georgie. "I'm the one who got drained, after all."

Ermin wanted to tear her hair out in frustration. "We've already discussed this!"

"It wouldn't be that hard for you to switch places," said Colin.

Why was he supporting Georgie? What was wrong with him? "Can we please just stick to the plan?"

"Only your roles will change," said Colin. "The plan stays the same. You can easily trade the transpositor for the smoke bombs once you're safely inside. Georgie's the one who got hurt. Doesn't she deserve a chance to get even?"

Georgie did deserve that chance. The only trouble was,

Ermin had come to think of the transpositor as her own creation and secretly hated the idea of handing it over to anyone else, especially someone as impulsive as Georgie. Ermin had taken it apart and rebuilt it, making a completely new machine out of the bones of the old. Her entire future depended on that machine. What if Georgie dropped it? Colin and Georgie looked at her expectantly, waiting for an answer.

"All right," she grudgingly conceded. "We'll switch over once we're inside. But no more changes, all right?"

"Agreed," said Georgie.

"Oh, I almost forgot," said Colin. "Denny gave me a necklace that he says belongs to you. He claims that he found it outside in the yard. Or maybe he doesn't know how to tell a certain mechanic how much he likes her."

Ermin was beyond relieved to discover that Denny had found the necklace. "Don't you start! Miss Fetchkeep gave that necklace to me, not Denny." She must have dropped it outside, after all. "You'd better keep it for now. I don't want to risk it falling out of my pocket again."

"Don't worry. I'll keep Darling Denny's gift safe," Colin said with a grin.

The gate squeaked open. Frank Price, the owner of the hotel, stood on the threshold. A woman wearing a rubber smock stood behind him, brandishing a large tube of Sifton's Louse Bane. Her hair was drawn back in a bun so tight, her entire face looked stretched.

"Come in, come in, everyone!" said Frank, rubbing his hands together. "If you follow Mrs. Brack, she'll make sure you're sorted out."

Mrs. Brack's lips pursed, as if she hardly relished the task. As Ermin and Georgie passed through the gate, she depressed the tube's plunger. A white cloud of louse bane rose up and settled over them. Frank coughed loudly. In the yard, a double row of troughs had been set up. Most of the street kids hung back. Water was not a welcome sight.

"Wash your hands and faces at the troughs—with soap!" Mrs. Brack said. "And feet too, for those without shoes. Extra masks are inside on the table. Follow the corridor straight through to the kitchen—and don't go anywhere else."

Ermin and Georgie ran for the nearest trough to soap up before the water became too dirty.

"You two with the masks, wash your faces," Mrs. Brack commanded.

Ermin splashed soapy water up underneath her mask. She had no intention of removing it. A back door stood open, leading into the bowels of the hotel. Still dripping, Ermin and Georgie made their way inside with the other washed recruits. They found a table laid out with spare masks, just as Mrs. Brack had said.

One of the girls rolled her eyes at the sight of them. "Why do we have to wear these? We've got immunity to the fever."

"The toffs don't," said a boy, tugging a mask down over his face. "They think the likes of us are spreading nasty germs."

"Notice how they've saved all the plain ones for us?" said another. "You can bet they're all eagles and falcons out there."

Ermin and Georgie dallied at the edges of the room until the rest of the recruits had filed through. When the last one strapped on a mask and disappeared down the hall, Georgie poked her head out into the yard.

"They're just barring the gate. Lucky we showed up when we did. There's plenty of kids on the other side who didn't make it in. Uh-oh. Mrs. Brack's heading this way. We'd better go."

They hastened along an L-shaped corridor. A cacophony of banging pans and voices grew louder as they neared the kitchen, where a line of stragglers waited outside. Ermin's stomach fluttered. She and Georgie were supposed to creep past the kitchen unseen. That would be impossible now. She wondered about reversing direction but changed her mind when she heard the purposeful click of boot heels behind them. She and Georgie pushed past the line of kids.

"Where do you think you're going?" one of them yelled.

The click of pursuing heels sped up. "Stop this instant!" Mrs. Brack shouted.

Ermin and Georgie broke into a run. Their best hope was to get into position before Mrs. Brack nabbed them or, failing that, to find a good hiding place until the fuss died down. The corridor took a turn to the right—toward the front of the hotel.

"You two!" Mrs. Brack called. "Come back!"

Ermin and Georgie ran for all they were worth. A black curtain loomed ahead. They pushed through it and found themselves in the great hall. The corridor must be a service passage, where food could be brought in from the kitchen and empty platters whisked away behind the curtain.

The room was breathtaking.

Boughs of hemlock, spruce, and white pine hung down from the rafters and draped the pillars. More boughs had been arranged in bristling clumps, to make it look as though trees were growing through the walls. Lamps winked and shone, nestled in the greenery. A cloud of butterflies flitted past. One caught in Ermin's cloak, its wings beating helplessly with a mechanical whir. It was a clockwork butterfly, made of tin. She plucked it off and flipped it over, taking note of the minute gears and tiny jointed legs until Georgie plucked at her sleeve.

"No, you can't take that apart right now. Come on!"

Reluctantly, Ermin released it.

The butterfly whirred off toward a semicircular stage backed by red and gold curtains. Musicians were already making their way onto it with instrument cases and sheet music. Red and gold painted pennants unfurled in opposite directions above the stage to encircle the room, joining together above a fireplace set into the opposite wall. A horseshoe-shaped upper gallery ran around the room, with a staircase leading up to it. They headed for it, and not a moment too soon. The black curtain jerked open and Mrs. Brack stood there, raking the room with angry eyes.

Georgie gripped her arm. She wasn't looking at Mrs. Brack but down at the floor. The thick pine boards had been painted to look like the storm-tossed waters of the Great Lake. The effect was so realistic, Ermin felt as if the next step she took would plunge her headfirst into water.

"This blasted floor looks so real, I almost feel seasick," Georgie muttered. "I wish to blazes I'd never looked down."

Ermin threaded her arm through Georgie's. "Come on, we're nearly there."

Nobody stopped them as they grabbed trays and walked across the floor and up the stairs. Then again, they were servers. Nobody paid attention to servers. The railings of the upper gallery were so thick with boughs, it was hard to find a place to see through. They finally located a spot above the stage. The musicians were now warming up. Bows scraped across strings with a deafening screech, and horns and flutes trilled up and down, running through their scales. Mrs. Brack was nowhere to be seen. Frank Price strode into the hall carrying a chain, which he fastened on either side of the stairs to close off access to the gallery.

"That was close," said Georgie. "Give me the transpositor."

Ermin suddenly remembered how careless Georgie could be.

She unstrapped the transpositor and held it close. Her uneasiness about handing over the transpositor was growing worse by the minute. She could hardly bring herself to let it go.

"See this yellow dial? It's the on-off switch. You've got to make sure you point the draining lamp at D'Arcy. I've notched the wood underneath the *fill* end so you can tell the two apart."

"Off, on, draining end, notches," Georgie rattled off. She held out her hands for the transpositor.

"No!" Ermin kept a firm grip on the transpositor. "It's the *unnotched* end you want to point at D'Arcy. Don't point the notched end at him, whatever you do."

"Does it matter? It's not as if I can give him any more power."

"But you can."

"How?"

Ermin closed her eyes. This mission was nerve-racking enough without giving out extra instructions. "The orange orbulet is still inside the machine. I didn't want to leave it lying around for Denny to find."

"So why don't you just put it in your pocket?"

"Because it fizzes and pops like anything once it's disconnected. Look, if this is too hard for you... "

Georgie grabbed the transpositor. "I said I'd do it, all right? Here are the bombs." She handed six oblong pellets to Ermin. "Make sure you don't lob them in all at once. Only three at a time. Wait for two minutes after the first three, then toss in the rest. That should make enough smoke to cover our tracks."

Guests filed into the hall. Ermin wondered if the smoke would give them enough time to push their way through a stampeding crowd all heading for the exit at the same time. "Don't let go of the transpositor, not even for a second!"

"I'm hardly going to leave it lying around for the Magistrates to find, am I? Look, Governor Hawking's just arrived."

Governor Maitland Hawking entered the great hall wearing a white wig, a black frock coat, and an eagle's mask, with the Governor's medallion hung around his neck. Guests bowed their heads as he threaded his way through the assembled throng. Beside him walked a woman in a resplendent green frock coat, trousers, and a top hat. A cat's mask peeked out from beneath its emerald brim. People paraded through the hall in their finery, brilliant hues shifting in a kaleidoscope of living color. White lace frothed from cuffs and spilled in snowy ruffles from the fronts of jackets. Everyone wore conical masks elaborately decorated to make them look like predatory birds or animals. Clouds of mechanical butterflies whirred around the room.

"It's like a blasted menagerie down there," said Georgie. "Let's go."

Ermin didn't feel even remotely ready. Now that they were deep inside the hotel, their plan seemed to be riddled with holes. What if the smoke bombs didn't work and they got nabbed?

Georgie, however, seemed to harbor no doubts as she hastened down the stairs. Ermin experienced a surge of sudden misgiving as she ducked under the chain. She hadn't checked to make sure that Georgie had strapped on the transpositor correctly, with the draining side up. It was too late to do anything about it. She made her way to the fireplace, fingering the bombs in her pocket and trying to quell her rising sense of panic. The room swelled with guests. She'd lost sight of Georgie. How was she supposed to know when to throw in the first smoke bombs if she couldn't tell whether Georgie had found her target or not? The obvious answer was to find D'Arcy first, yet she had to remain near the fireplace. *Hold steady, girl.* Even if she couldn't see them, she would certainly hear the sound of a commotion. She cradled the first batch of bombs in her fist, waiting for Georgie to strike.

Chapter Fourteen

Ermin hadn't been standing at her post for long when one of the servers came up and thrust a tray at her. Ermin was so startled, she nearly dropped the bombs she'd been holding.

"Do you mind?" the girl said, shaking the tray. Something about her tone was familiar but Ermin couldn't see her face, obscured as it was behind a plain white mask. "I've got to go back for more."

"More? But you haven't handed these around yet."

"You can do that."

The girl pushed the tray at Ermin, who had no choice but to grab it before it spilled. The sudden motion dislodged one of the smoke bombs from her hand. It fell to the floor. Ermin tried to cover it up with her foot, but it was too late. The girl had seen it. She stared at Ermin over the top of her mask.

"Who are you?" the girl asked.

This time, there was no mistaking the voice. "Essey?"

Before the girl could answer, a crowd of hungry partygoers descended on them. Hand after hand grabbed at the tray. By the time Ermin had extricated herself, the girl was gone. She was sure that the voice had belonged to Essey, but why would a seasoned apprentice hire herself out to Frank Price? Ermin couldn't very well rush after the girl in search of answers. She had to remain at her post. The real question was, what was she going to do with this tray?

"You." A bony woman wearing a swan mask snapped her fingers at Ermin, her voice petulant. "Over here."

She was one of many who sat on chairs set up around the edges of the room. Ermin hesitated. If she went over to where the woman was sitting, she'd definitely be out of range of the fireplace. She'd also dropped one of the bombs. That little mistake had cost them some precious getaway time. How much more time would it cost them if she couldn't get back to the fire in time to throw in the remaining bombs?

"You!" Swan Woman snapped her fingers again. "Over here, I say!"

Ermin swore inwardly. Why couldn't the woman choose one of the other servers? She knew the answer. The woman didn't like being disobeyed and felt compelled to remind Ermin of her status. She would only get louder and more insistent, and that would attract unwanted attention. She dragged herself forward, keeping her eyes peeled for signs of Georgie.

"It's about time," Swan Woman complained. "Another minute and I'd have gone straight to Frank Price himself. You'd best remember your place, girl, or I'll have you thrown out."

Heat rushed into Ermin's face. She longed to dump the tray's contents straight into Swan Woman's lap, but that gesture would ruin more than her dress. She forced her voice to assume a contrite tone. "Yes, ma'am. Sorry, ma'am."

Another woman, wearing a goldfinch mask, sat beside Swan Woman and fanned herself with a large leaf she'd plucked from one of the nearby plants. She languished in her seat as if the very act of breathing was too arduous.

Swan Woman snatched a cracker-y blob off the tray, dangling it between thumb and forefinger. "What is this?" she asked with a shiver of disgust.

Ermin hadn't the faintest idea. "A cracker?" All she could think about was getting back to the fireplace.

Swan Woman glared at Ermin. "Don't be impertinent!"

"The servants these days are all impertinent and lazy," Goldfinch complained. "Even the indentured ones. My Hetty, whose passage I paid for out of my own pocket, once called me a 'prune-mouthed old nag' because I pointed out the flaws in her silver polishing."

Swan Woman clucked her tongue sympathetically.

"Of course, I dismissed her without a reference, but the brazen hussy had no shame. She started her own grist mill... with an immigrant!"

"You're not talking about Hetty Chen, are you?" Swan Woman asked, astounded.

"The very one," Goldfinch replied darkly.

Ermin was so surprised, she almost dropped the tray. A green-suited woman in a cat mask appeared at her side and steadied the tray with a sure hand.

"Hetty and Soon-Yi's flours are quite excellent," the cat-masked woman cut in smoothly. "Maitland and I use them in our own household, as does Queen Georgina."

Swan Woman gave a violent start. "Rachel Hawking, is that you? Indeed, I did not recognize you behind your mask."

Rachel Hawking, the Governor's wife, took the tray from Ermin, giving her a wink from behind her transparent eye guard. "Thank you, my dear."

Ermin hastened back to the fireplace, only to discover that a group of people had parked themselves in front of it. Not just any people, either, but top-brass Magistrates, judging from their purple neckties with silver insignia. A portly ginger-haired man stretched his hands out to the flames, as though to claim all the warmth for himself. His conical mask had been blunted to resemble the rounded snout of a lion, its mouth painted open in a roar. Ermin would bet that it was Dr. Dean, Chief Magistrate of Garrison Creek. Two figures stood to either side of him. Ermin recognized the one in the wolf mask instantly as Chief Controller Gerrard Shuter.

A wave of hatred surged through her. Shuter had orchestrated the mass drainings at Redemption Square. It had been his idea to use the wizards' stolen power to fuel the sun lamps dotted over every farmer's field—and to charge them a hefty price for it too. On the other side of Dr. Dean stood Vice Regent Ferguson Briggs, his second-in-command, who'd donned the mask of a brindled wolverine. Ermin stared at his sleek, black helmet of hair and wondered if he'd used shellac to hold it in place. Three of the most powerful figures in the Creek, assembled right before her. Her knees threatened to give way. She managed to retreat behind a group of potted plants before she collapsed. The full insanity of their plan rained down on her. How had they ever thought they could take on the assembled might of the Magistrates and win?

She tried to slow her breathing. Georgie was still out there. She had no idea that the Creek's three most powerful Magistrates had effectively blocked Ermin from carrying out her part of the plan. Ermin had to find some way to warn her. But how?

Just then, a woman clad in a sparkling silver gown and silver mask glided toward the Magistrates. She uttered a low, croaking laugh as Shuter bent over her hand.

"Ah, Miss Fetchkeep," he murmured. "Delighted."

Ermin crouched down, terrified that Miss Fetchkeep would recognize her again. An emaciated man wearing a black conical mask materialized at Miss Fetchkeep's elbow, swaying on his feet.

"Is that you, D'Arcy?" Shuter asked as he straightened. "I hardly recognize you. Are you ill?"

D'Arcy didn't look at all well. The mask he wore dwarfed his head, and his hands twitched constantly.

"Ill? Not with the fever, I hope!" Dr. Dean scuttled backward in alarm.

"No, Chief Magistrate," replied Miss Fetchkeep. "It's just a case of overwork, nothing more."

"Has he been tested?" Briggs asked as he and Shuter planted themselves in front of the Chief Magistrate.

"He has, and the results were negative," said Miss Fetchkeep. "It's not the fever. There's no cause for alarm."

"I'm quite well," rasped D'Arcy. "Indeed, I'm quite recovered."

Recovered, my foot, thought Ermin. D'Arcy looked like a wizard caught in the grip of blowback. He must have burned through the power he'd stolen from Georgie, and without the transpositor he had no way of replenishing it. It seemed he'd become addicted to it.

D'Arcy drew himself up to his full height so that he towered over Briggs, who'd instinctively stepped forward to intercept him. "I'm no danger to the Chief Magistrate, Briggs. Step aside."

"I don't take my orders from you, D'Arcy." Briggs's voice was quiet and dangerous.

"Come now, Briggs! There's no need for that," Dr. Dean said. "We're all friends here."

If looks could skewer, D'Arcy would be dead. Reluctantly, Briggs stepped aside.

"You haven't been at one of your experiments again, have you, D'Arcy?" Dr. Dean asked. D'Arcy didn't answer. "Good gracious, man! Wasn't losing your position enough without risking your new situation?"

If Dr. Dean thought he was helping matters with this public reprimand, he was sorely mistaken. D'Arcy clenched his fists so tightly, his knuckles turned white.

Miss Fetchkeep laid a steadying hand on D'Arcy's arm. "Never forget how indispensable you are to the school, Mr. D'Arcy. St. Anselm's would fall apart without you."

"Thank you, ma'am," D'Arcy said through gritted teeth. "It is astonishing to me that a society that holds magi-tech in such reverence should be so hostile toward scientific experimentation. I've come to inform you that I've discovered a power that could completely transform our settlement. You were quite wrong to dismiss me, Chief Magistrate."

"Indeed?" Shuter exchanged a coy half smile with Briggs. "And how do you—a self-taught magi-technician—propose to 'transform' our settlement?"

"Perhaps you should complete your degree at the new college first before making such boastful claims, D'Arcy," said Briggs. "That is, if they'll admit you."

D'Arcy ripped off his mask. "Then allow me to show you!" There were a few startled gasps as the surrounding people shrank away from the group. The situation was getting out of control. *Come on, Georgie.*

"How dare you?" Dr. Dean croaked. "Do you want to infect us all? Put on your mask at once!"

"I don't need a mask to protect me from tree fever, Chief Magistrate, because I am immune to it. All thanks to my experiments."

"Experiments... immunity? What are you talking about, man?"

"Ignore him, Chief Magistrate," said Briggs. "His boasts clearly had no effect, so now he must resort to lies."

"Lies, is it?" D'Arcy advanced on Ferguson Briggs until he stood toe to toe with the Vice Regent. Briggs held his ground, his back rigid with fear and fury. Very slowly, D'Arcy opened his hand to reveal a small brown flame dancing on his palm.

Briggs shrank back in horror. "That's an abomination!"

Ermin wasn't sure how many other guests had witnessed D'Arcy's conjurement because Georgie chose that moment to break through the crowd, brandishing the transpositor. People started pushing for the exit with startled cries. Georgie twisted the yellow dial, her face set in an expression of grim satisfaction as the blast hit D'Arcy square in the chest. Briggs and Shuter dove at Dr. Dean, trying to cover him with their bodies. The magician let out a cry and dropped to his knees, his face contorted with pain or fury, Ermin didn't know which. Georgie stood alone to confront him.

Ermin broke cover and raced over to the fireplace. D'Arcy rose to his feet so fast, he almost levitated. This was not how she'd expected a drained wizard to behave. Georgie must have fired from the wrong end. Instead of draining D'Arcy, the transpositor had filled him up with new wizardry! Georgie must have realized this herself because she hastily switched off the machine. Ermin hurled all of the smoke bombs into the flames at once. Seconds later, a series of loud explosions rocked the room. Ermin pitched forward onto her hands and knees. The startled cries turned to screams as the rest of the crowd rushed for the exits. White clouds of smoke billowed into the room— too much of it to have come from a handful of smoke bombs.

Briggs and Shuter pulled Dr. Dean to his feet. "Get the Chief Magistrate out of here and arm yourselves! We're under attack!"

There was a mad scramble as Magistrates dressed in sparkling finery pushed against the the growing stampede, heading to the cloakroom to retrieve their bewitchers.

Georgie hauled Ermin up by the arm. "Come on, we've got to get out of here!"

With a terrible screech, D'Arcy stepped in front of them to block their path. Ermin watched in horror as his head began to grow, bulging outward in a series of pulsating expansions. Four red eyes popped out of his forehead like blisters. His fingers fused together, then lengthened into two reedy, sticklike prongs. A set of mandibles burst from his mouth, clicking together in agitation. The creature uttered a piercing shrill. A blast of pink goo shot out of his insect mouth, heading straight for them. Before it could strike, a woman in a green suit stepped in front of them holding out a metal tray like a shield.

"Run!" Rachel Hawking shouted as pink goo splatted against the tray. The sizzle of melting metal rang in Ermin's ears as she and Georgie sprang away.

"Blasted embers!" Georgie squeaked. "He's turned himself into a monster!"

He already is a monster, Ermin wanted to say, but she had no breath left to speak. She and Georgie rounded the stage and tore through the black curtain. They dashed down the serving corridor, past a group of startled servers. The insect magician's screeches echoed behind them.

"What's going on out here?" Mrs. Brack shouted, emerging from the kitchen. "Come back at once, or you'll not get a single penny—" She screamed as a mouthful of pink goo landed on the wall.

Ermin and Georgie pelted into the yard and ran for the gate. As soon as they were through, Georgie wedged a heavy log in front of it.

"Where's Colin?"

Ermin cast her eyes to the sky, but all she could see were gray clouds. "Maybe he's gone around to the front."

They raced around to the front of the hotel. Broken glass

crunched underfoot. Screams and bangs erupted through the shattered panes. The front doors had been torn off their hinges by the panicked crowd. Clouds of silvery-white smoke from bewitchers drifted through the opening. The surrounding street was full of fleeing guests. Most were on foot, though some had had the presence of mind to snatch up their flying cloaks and carpets. Colin was nowhere to be seen. Magistrates flew from upstairs windows and circled the hotel in a protective formation, their bewitchers at the ready as they scanned the crowd.

Georgie eyed them fearfully. "They'll be looking for me. We've got to get out of here."

"No, they're not. They're looking for that monster, D'Arcy..."

" ...and the person who turned him into one. To anyone watching, that's what it looked like."

The horrible truth of this sank into Ermin. "Get rid of your mask. It will be one less thing for them to recognize."

They abandoned their masks and moved away from the hotel. Ermin cast a swift glance over her shoulder. D'Arcy had just come around the corner of the hotel. He shrilled at the sight of them and clawed at the air with his hooked prongs. Two Magistrates swooped down to engage him while the others spread out in ever-widening circles over the crowd. Ermin's legs wobbled, as if they might give out again. How would they ever get away without Colin and the carpet? It was just one more thing that had gone wrong—only this mistake might very well prove to be fatal.

There was a swirl of brown and black as Georgie shifted shape. Nobody paid her any mind, maybe because the trans-positor that Georgie still wore bore a passing resemblance to a spell-casting bewitcher. Georgie's webbed feet smacked down on Ermin's shoulders and she gave an urgent hiss. Ermin grabbed hold of Georgie's goose legs and began to run as Georgie's strong goose wings beat the air. The propulsion from each wingbeat lengthened Ermin's stride and lent her a swiftness she otherwise never could have achieved. Around them, more and more people fired off their own bewitchers, adding to the confusion. Meanwhile, D'Arcy calmly picked off the airborne Magistrates with well-aimed shots of pink goo while he continued to pursue Ermin and Georgie.

"The Magistrates can't stop him," said Ermin.

Georgie gave a fearful honk. Her wings beat with a fresh burst of speed as she veered north along the Old North Road. D'Arcy's screeches grew fainter with every wing-borne step Ermin took. *Good.* The more distance they could put between themselves and the insect magician, the more time they had to come up with an alternate plan for how to throw him off for good. Going up against D'Arcy in his current form was suicide.

Georgie didn't stop flying until they were so far up the Old North Road, they were nearly in the countryside. Mr. Jesse's tannery was the Creek's last outpost, located far away from the settlement because of its dreadful smell. Ermin let go of Georgie's legs, and collapsed against the fence. Georgie rematerialized from her goose shape and sank down beside her.

"I need a rest. Phew!" she said, holding her nose. "I'd forgotten how bad this place smells."

The air from the yard was so pungent that Ermin had to breathe through her mouth. A broadside pasted to the fence read:

Highest prices paid. Puer collected at all times when notice
is left
at the Tannery. Boots patched in exchange, if required.

"Remember the time the three of us collected dog dung for Mr. Jesse?" Georgie said.

"Do I ever!" Before half a day was up, Ermin had asked Mr. Jesse how much he'd pay them to piss into the bating vats instead. The only payments they'd received that day were a couple of hard clouts to the ear. She would have welcomed a clout from Mr. Jesse now. At least it would mean that he was here. "What do you think happened to Colin?"

Georgie's brow creased. "I don't know. D'Arcy couldn't have gotten to him because he was inside with us. Colin would never have ditched us, not unless he was forced to. Not that I think that anything bad happened to him," she added hastily. "Maybe things got too hot for him. He's probably waiting for us back at Denny's." She cocked her head to one side.

"What is it?" Ermin couldn't hear anything, but then again she didn't have a wizard's ears.

"It's that insect creature," said Georgie. "I can hear it screeching away down the road."

"How does he know where we are?"

"I don't know. Maybe he's following our smell." Georgie turned to Ermin with a despairing gaze. "I don't think I can fly anymore."

Ermin's arms and legs ached. She doubted she'd be able to run much farther herself. A particularly foul stench wafted through the fence. Maybe she didn't have to. "What if we mask our smell by hiding out at the tannery?"

"Blasted embers, but you're brilliant! Quick, let's hop the fence. He's getting nearer."

Ermin took the fence at a running jump, hooking her hands and the heel of one boot over the top boards to pull herself over the fence and into the yard where mounds of puer, or dog dung, lay heaped about in piles. Georgie landed beside her, cupping her nose and mouth. Ermin ran over to the nearest tanning shed. Some of the windows had missing panes. Mr. Jesse hadn't bothered to replace them, making it easy for Ermin and Georgie to crawl through and lower themselves into the dim interior. The inside of the shed was just as disgusting as the outside. Lime pits were sunk along the length of the flagstone floor. Even worse were the bating vats, where leather hides were soaked in a putrid mixture of urine and puer. The workers, dressed in drawers and not much else, would stomp the hides into softness with their bare feet.

The pits were too open to offer much of a hiding place. The insect D'Arcy would spot them in an instant. She peered over the edge of the nearest bating vat. A foul-smelling liquid sloshed around inside, the ammonia strong enough to make her eyes water. She couldn't bring herself to climb inside. That left the tanning drums, which were used for tumbling the hides to get as much moisture out of them as possible before they were stretched on racks to dry. Ermin lifted the hinged top on one of the drums. The inside stank but it was mostly dry. She and Georgie climbed in, coughing and choking. The drum's hinges groaned under their combined weight.

"I just hope it doesn't break," said Georgie.

"It won't," Ermin said with more confidence than she felt as she closed the lid. The movement made the drum rock back and forth.

She opened the lid a crack so she could peer out. She heard the insect magician's clicking and hissing long before its frightful silhouette appeared at the window. It hooked its prongs over an empty frame and swung itself through. Once inside, it began to examine its surroundings, systematically peering inside each lime pit and bating vat in turn. The creature let out a screech of fury every time it found one empty. With a growing horror, Ermin watched as it made its way toward the tanning drum where they were hiding.

"What's going on in there?" a gruff male voice called out.

It must be the night watcher, aroused by all the noise. A chain clanked. The lock on the shed door rattled. The insect magician's mandibles worked. A splatter of pink froth hit the ground by the door, smoking. The night watcher would be incinerated as soon as he stepped inside.

"Keep away!" Ermin cried out. She closed the lid entirely, hoping that the creature wouldn't be able to pinpoint her whereabouts.

A triumphant screech told her just how vain that hope had been.

"Keep away, is it, you young ruffian?" the night watcher said. "Come away from there or you'll answer to my cudgel."

The tanning drum shook, as if from a blow, then a hole made by drizzling pink foam appeared directly in front of Ermin's face. Through the new hole, she saw the insect magician's mandibles working fiercely to produce another shot. She flung open the lid and dropped to the ground. Georgie's boots thumped the ground behind her.

"Don't come in!" Ermin yelled to the night watcher.

"Mr. Jesse doesn't pay protection to you thugs so you can double-cross him behind his back!" A large man lumbered into view, the light from his lantern reflecting off his bald pate. The insect magician chittered excitedly, rubbing its prongs together in eager anticipation.

"Embers preserve us!" the night watcher cried.

The insect magician lunged, but Ermin and Georgie were quicker. They slammed into the watcher, knocking him over just as a pair of mandibles scissored over the place where his neck had been. Georgie jumped and aimed a furious kick at the creature's shins. "Take that, ugly jugs!"

The creature yowled in pain. Georgie took off, running in a zigzag pattern through the shed. The creature sprang after her.

Georgie knocked over a bating vat. A stinking liquid sloshed out, drenching the creature in foulness. It slipped and fell, screeching in fury. Whether Georgie was brave or foolish, Ermin didn't know, but she'd created enough of a distraction to get the watcher away.

She grabbed his hand and pulled. He lumbered to his feet, gripping her hand tightly. Together, they ran through the yard. They didn't stop until they reached the gate, where the watcher released her. "Thank you, lass. I'm going to fetch the Magistrates. I'll say nothing about you, so make sure you and your friend are gone before I get back." He charged through the gate, as if the monster were still after him.

A part-goose Georgie flew through a window and banked as the insect creature emerged. She beat him over the head with her wings, then flew off, banking and rolling to avoid the blasts of pink goo he fired after her. The transpositor was still strapped to her chest. All Ermin had to do was to buy her enough time to use it.

"Yah, ugly jugs!" Ermin taunted. "If that pink goo is the best you can do, maybe you should go back to school!"

The insect D'Arcy let out an ear-piercing screech. It seemed to be every bit as touchy about its lack of formal education as the human D'Arcy. It turned away from Georgie and raced toward Ermin at a terrible speed, mandibles clicking ferociously. Ermin's heart jumped into her throat. She ran, her legs stumbling in panic. Goo spattered against the fence, eating through the wood where it struck. She pelted around the corner of the tanning shed only to find her way blocked by a dead end. She whirled just as the insect D'Arcy came into view. Its four red eyes were fixed on her. This was it, Ermin realized. She was going to die.

Georgie landed behind the creature, transforming herself back into a human. She aimed the draining end of the transpositor at the creature and fired. It rocked backward on its stick legs, caught in the current.

"See how you like it!" Georgie shouted. She kept the transpositor trained on the creature, draining away its energy, but instead of collapsing as Georgie had done, the creature started to shrink, its prongs clawing at the air feebly. "Why is it changing size?"

"I don't know. Maybe it has something to do with the conjurement he cast."

The creature continued to shrink until it was the size of a small praying mantis, then stopped. Georgie lowered the transpositor. The creature turned a tiny triangular face toward them. Without enough power to transform his own body back to its original form, D'Arcy could very easily be trapped inside this insect shape forever.

"Step on it," said Georgie.

"What?"

"Step on it. You're closer."

Ermin hesitated. It was one thing to defeat the creature D'Arcy had become, quite another thing to kill it. Taking advantage of her hesitation, the creature launched itself into the air. With a scrabble of claws and wings, it landed on a nearby drain.

"Quick, Ermin! Squash it before it gets away!"

Ermin raised her foot. Somehow, she couldn't bring herself to stomp down on that tiny face. With a tinny scrape of claws, the praying mantis squeezed through the grate and was gone.

Georgie came to stand beside her, staring down at the drain. "I probably couldn't have done it either. Besides, it's not as if he can drain any more wizards, can he? Not without his infernal machine."

"I don't think he can change back without it either."

Georgie turned a shining face toward Ermin. "We've done

it! We've finally defeated the old skeleton. He won't ever drain another wizard again. I can't wait to tell Colin!"

"If we ever find him."

"*When* we find him, gloomy guts. The sight of all those Magistrates flying in must have scared him away. He probably flew the carpet straight back to Denny's. That's where we'll find him." Georgie shrugged free of the transpositor, holding it out in front of her as if it might bite her. "Before we go, I'm going to dump this menace into the nearest bating vat."

"You can't!" Ermin wrenched the machine away from Georgie. "Not after all the modifications I made."

"Don't tell me you're actually planning to use it again? That tube is still half-full of some drained wizard's essence. Nobody has the right to use it for anything."

"I'm not talking about using any drained wizard's essence! I want to study the machine. What if it could be modified in some way to protect wizards? It can be used for good—I know it can."

"Used for good?" Georgie was horrified. "That machine's pure evil. What if it falls into the wrong hands? It has to be destroyed."

"No, it doesn't."

"You'll never be able to keep it once we join the Resistance. I'd never let you bring it anywhere near them."

Arrows of anger shot through Ermin. Who was Georgie to decide what she could and couldn't do? She hadn't done all this work only to have it tossed away like it meant nothing. "I'm not joining the Resistance."

Georgie stared at her, speechless.

"I'm not going to indenture myself to a bunch of wizards who can't tell a screw from a nail. I'm going to spend the winter working for Denny and figuring out how to use the transpositor for good. As soon as I do, I'm going to present it to the Guild.

Then they'll have to accept me as a student." She hadn't meant to say this last bit out loud, but she was so angry that the words slipped out.

Georgie's eyes flashed. "So you're willing to betray us for a place in the Guild?"

"I've never betrayed you or Colin, or any wizard, and I never will. You know that."

Purple sparks flew from Georgie's fingers. "I could destroy the machine right now."

"Go ahead." Ermin wrapped her arms tightly around the transpositor. "Only a traitor would fire on a friend."

She found herself confronted by an angry goose. With a soft hiss, the goose arched her neck and spread two gigantic black and brown wings. For a minute Ermin thought that Georgie was going to attack her, but she didn't. Instead, Georgie leapt into the air. She was airborne in two wingbeats. With a cacophony of honks that Ermin imagined were the goose's equivalent of swear words, Georgie circled the tanner's yard, then flew south toward the lake, to where a line of smoke puddled on the horizon like spilled ink.

Ermin fell back against the wall. A lone feather drifted down from the sky and landed in front of her. She felt completely empty inside. She and Georgie had butted heads plenty of times before, but there was a kind of finality to this fight that frightened her. How could Georgie ever think that Ermin would turn on her? The machine wasn't evil; it was only a tool, one that had fallen right into her lap. Why couldn't Georgie understand the opportunity it represented? She hadn't thought the machine was bad when Ermin had used it to restore her power, proving that it could be used for other purposes. It wasn't fair of her to deny Ermin the chance to study it further.

A second frightening thought struck her. Would Colin turn

against her too? She still might be able to talk him around if she could get back to the forge before Georgie poisoned his mind against her. She had to make him see that she wasn't his enemy, that they were still on the same side. Then maybe, just maybe, he might be able to convince Georgie too.

She dragged herself to her feet. The beginnings of a headache throbbed inside her skull. She needed to muster every last ounce of strength for the long trek back to Denny's. It would take her straight through the heart of Wharf Rat territory. As always, the Rat King and his minions would be watching.

Chapter Fifteen

arkness had settled like a nightmare over Old Town. Thick clouds blanketed the moon and fog swirled underfoot, making it hard to see. The street lamps were little more than dim yellow globes that did nothing to dispel the swirling mist. Ermin headed in the direction of St. Andrew's market. It was a risky route, but speed was of the essence. The Rats would most likely be out in full force, but Ermin was counting on making herself hard to find. The market was filled with revelers who couldn't afford the price of admission to the Magistrates' Ball but had decided to stage their own party outside. With any luck, she'd find a mark heading in the direction of Denny's.

She cast a quick glance up at the rooftops. She was relieved to find only empty sky, no huddled heads watching her. The only whistles and calls she heard were from enterprising news hawkers. She drew closer as a man stopped to buy a paper. He snapped on a light stitched into the brim of his cap, shining it over the papers. Ermin stepped close and craned her neck over his shoulder to read.

WIZARD ATTACK ON MAGISTRATES' BALL, screamed the headline. FRANK'S HOTEL BOMBED!

Ermin remembered the explosion shaking the floor under her feet. Five measly smoke bombs couldn't have produced a blast like that, nor the thick cloud of smoke she'd seen from the tannery. There must have been a second explosion from a real bomb. To think that the Resistance had been so close all that time! Georgie must be tearing her hair out with frustration. Or her feathers. She wondered if Georgie had flown back to the hotel, in hopes of meeting them. If so, she wouldn't have had a chance to talk to Colin yet. Ermin might be able to get to him first, if she hurried.

The mark folded his paper and started off down the street, in the opposite direction to where Ermin was going. It started to snow. Ermin looked up. If she took to the roofs, she could be at Denny's in no time. A rain barrel stood a few paces off. Should she chance it? There were still plenty of people about, not that any of them would risk tangling with Rory's Rats.

A rush of snow hit her face. She stuck out her tongue, feeling the cold flare of each flake as it landed. It seemed like a signal. A little boy ran past her. He wore an oversized peacoat with an oversized muffler wound about his head. Even so, Ermin would have recognized him anywhere.

"Mouse!" she called out.

Mouse stopped and turned around. He stood staring at her, chewing on the fringed end of his muffler. A shadow passed over Ermin's head. In the next instant, the looped end of a rope passed over her head, pinning her arms to her sides. She tried to jerk free but her attacker cinched the rope tight. She was caught.

"Run, Mouse!" she shouted.

Mouse didn't move. He stood there, biting his scarf and staring as her assailant dragged her back into the shadows. A group of revelers danced past, holding torches. Golden light slid across her captor's face long enough for Ermin to be able to tell who it was.

"Snarl!" Ermin gasped. "What are you doing?"

"Trying to trade the bounty Rory put on your head for the one he put on mine. I'm sorry, Ermin. Really I am, but this is the only way to make sure that he leaves me and Mouse alone."

Mouse drifted to her side. Even under several layers of clothes, his arms and legs still looked stick thin. He stared up at Ermin with eyes that were too big for his face, his nose a dripping red knob. Rory would never forgive Snarl, no matter what she thought. He was twisted enough to punish her in the way it would hurt the most—through Mouse. The thought of what Rory might do to him made Ermin feel sick.

"What makes you think he'll leave you alone after you turn me in? He'll never let you go, ever. Give me to Rory and you'll only be turning yourself in. Then what will happen to Mouse?"

Snarl chewed on her lip, her eyes darting anxiously back and forth over the crowds, as if she was either looking for Rory or weighing her chances of getting away. What if Ermin gave her a place to run to?

"I'm staying with Denny Lorde over at Smith's forge. I can take you there. He's looking for workers. You'll be safe with him."

Snarl chewed on her lip so fiercely, it began to bleed. As much as Ermin wanted to push her, she held back. She felt like Libra, balancing this moment on a set of mercurial scales. Push too hard in one direction and the scales might tip the other way.

A rectangular shadow detached itself from the darkness and swooped toward them at an unnatural speed. Ermin saw the pale flash of a face, fused front teeth bared in a snarl.

"Run!" she cried.

With a cry, Snarl grabbed Mouse's coat sleeve and jerked

him out of range of Rory's grasping fingers. The fingers swiped again, instantly getting knotted up in the wild strands of Ermin's hair. Tears sprang to her eyes as Rory gave a vicious tug.

"Got you!"

Chapter Sixteen

Ermin clawed at Rory. Knowing what was in store for her, she had nothing to lose by fighting back. Rory lifted her up by the hair and twisted her head around so she could witness Snarl and Mouse's escape. The sight of their two running figures filled Ermin with a defiant joy. Working for Denny would keep them safe. Rory would never be able to lay his hands on Mouse again.

Rory gave Ermin's hair another hard tug. Ermin clamped her lips shut to prevent herself from crying out. She wouldn't give Rory the satisfaction of knowing how much he was hurting her.

"Feast your eyes," Rory growled into her ear. "It's the last glimpse of freedom you'll ever have." He slammed her head down on the carpet. She recognized the worn phoenix pattern at once. It was her carpet, the one she'd fixed—the one she'd given to Colin.

Fire filled her lungs. If she was a wizard, she would have breathed fire all over Rory Smythe, incinerating him where he stood. "You filthy thief! What have you done to Colin?"

The sharp metal point of a knife pressed into her neck. "Any more of that, and you'll be tasting my blade. Got it?"

It wasn't like Rory to hold back, especially not when he was riled. The Rat King was famous throughout the Creek for his viciousness. Yet he'd stopped just short of cutting her. Why?

The pressure on her neck lessened. "Take her."

Two of Rory's Rats hauled her onto the carpet. Ermin recognized them as St. Anselm's students. The larger, more muscular of the two girls—Alice, her name was—smirked as she grabbed hold of the rope binding Ermin's arms, while her smaller companion, Twiggy, blinked at Ermin from behind thick glasses. Most people thought that Twiggy was the leader of the pair because her thick glasses made her look clever. Wily Alice worked hard to nurture that impression, but Ermin knew she was the real mastermind of the two. What were they doing with Rory? Had they left St. Anselm's to join the Rats? They were certainly mean enough to fit right in, although at the moment they both looked ill. Twiggy's face was positively green.

Rory leveled the knife at Ermin. "Try any funny business and I'll cut you."

Something was holding Rory back from exacting the revenge he so sorely wanted. That could only mean one thing: he needed something from her.

"Go ahead, stick me," she said. "You're going to, anyway."

Rory gestured to Twiggy and Alice. "Put that pillowcase over her head!"

Alice—or was it Twiggy?—dragged a pillowcase down over her face. It was made from the same rough hemp cloth they used at the school. With a series of bumpy jerks, the carpet ascended. The conviction inside Ermin grew. Rory hadn't killed her because she was useful to him. In what way, Ermin didn't know, but it bought her some time to come up with an escape plan. Her hands were still free. Best of all, she had the carpet back. All she had to do was figure out a way to get it away from Rory. That shouldn't be too hard. He could barely fly.

Forced down to her knees by Alice and Twiggy, Ermin gingerly edged forward on the carpet until her fingers touched the back of Rory's steer straps. They slapped against her hands as Rory flew. He hadn't bothered to fasten them. If she suddenly sprang forward and threw all of her weight against his back in one big push, he would topple off the carpet, leaving her in control. Except she'd still have Alice and Twiggy to deal with. Sick or not, Alice was still a formidable foe. Better not chance it.

Where was she? There was a small tear in the pillowcase, right around nose height. Contorting her face, she maneuvered the pillowcase around until her nose poked through the hole. The smells of horse dung, wet mud, and privies flowed by in a persistent current. The only thing she didn't smell was the lake. They were nowhere near the water or the *Lucky Charm*. Rory was taking her somewhere else.

Think, Ermin!

She racked her brains. A thin thread of memory unfurled: Chaser saying that St. Anselm's runaways were worth more to Rory. She couldn't forget the uncomfortable hints he'd dropped about Colin and Georgie. Did he know they were wizards? Did he suspect that Ermin was too? If so, then he might be trying to sell her. The bottom dropped out of her stomach, and it had nothing to do with Rory's driving. Was he taking her to the Fortress? That might explain why he was keeping her alive—to collect a bounty.

Her breath came out in panicked gasps. At the next lurch of the carpet, she pretended to lose her balance and sat back on her heels, readying her legs. She knew exactly where Rory was.

All she had to do was to hurl herself straight at him. Then she'd give Alice and Twiggy the ride of their lives.

A loud honk sounded overhead, followed by a beating of wings and a loud thump.

"Get off, you bleeding cawker!" Rory shouted.

The carpet veered to one side and took a plunge before rising up again at breakneck speed. With a scream, Alice dropped the rope. Instinctively, Ermin rose to a rider's crouch, wrenched her hands free and snatched off the pillowcase. It flew back, hitting Alice in the face. Even without any straps, she was practiced enough to ride the curves, her feet shifting direction with the carpet.

"Crouch down like I'm doing and stop fighting it!" she yelled to Rory. "You've got to ride out the turmoil until the carpet straightens. Jumping up and down will only make it worse."

Rory must have listened to her because the wild pitching died down. Bit by bit, the carpet leveled out.

"Put me down," Twiggy wailed. "I don't care about the money! I'll walk back to school."

"You'll get off when I decide," said Rory. "I'm not stopping until we get to where we're going."

"Quite right!" Alice agreed fervently. "What if that bird attacks us again?"

"So what if it does?" Rory blustered. "It's only a goose. Don't tell me you're afraid of an old goose?"

"You sure were," Alice mumbled.

Ermin cast a quick glance upward. She was certain it was Georgie who'd attacked Rory, which meant that she knew where Ermin was. Ermin couldn't see her in the dark, but that didn't mean that she wasn't there. Alice had somehow managed to hold on to the pillowcase in all the chaos. She made a feeble grab for Ermin but Ermin dropped to her knees, causing the carpet to respond with lightning speed. The three other riders cried out in fear.

"What are you two doing back there?" Rory shouted at Alice and Twiggy.

Ermin grabbed hold of Rory's heels, pulling up as she sprang to her feet. She let go as the carpet abruptly rose. Rory toppled over and fell to his knees. The carpet plummeted. Ermin dropped to a rider's crouch and leveled out the carpet just before it hit the cobblestones of Redemption Square. Alice and Twiggy both jumped off and ran.

"Come back here, you cowards!" Rory called out. "What will Miss Fetchkeep say?"

Ermin jumped off and seized the carpet in both hands. She gave it a violent wrench. Rory tumbled off, landing hard on his rear end. The carpet was hers! But before Ermin could fly away, two freezing-cold hands pressed down on her shoulders.

"Well played, Ermin," said Miss Fetchkeep.

Ermin stared at the headmistress in total shock. She still wore her shiny silver mask—the same one she'd worn at the ball. Her silver gown shimmered and glittered. Although she was wearing gloves, her grip was icy cold. Ermin's shoulders felt numb. Rory got to his feet so quickly that his silver-toed boots slid sideways on the rain-slicked cobbles. He reached for Ermin, but Miss Fetchkeep yanked her out of range.

"Wait a minute!" Rory protested. "We haven't settled up."

Miss Fetchkeep leaned forward until her silver-masked face loomed over Rory. "Not out here. We'll talk inside."

The Rat King did something Ermin had never seen him do: he scuttled backward like a frightened child. "We'll do more than talk," he blustered, his voice cracking.

Miss Fetchkeep said nothing as she led them toward a rectangular iron platform about ten feet high and twenty feet across. Ermin could see the shadowed outlines of four iron stakes with their loose chains clanking in the wind. It was the platform where they drained wizards of their power. At first it looked as if Miss Fetchkeep meant to lead them onto the platform, but at the last minute she turned aside. The ground beside the platform sloped abruptly down, leading around behind the small hill Redemption Square sat on. Ermin's and Rory's boots slipped on the wet cobbles, but Miss Fetchkeep never stumbled. She walked with a sliding grace, her spine held as straight as a sword. Ermin clasped the carpet to her chest. She must keep it away from Rory at all costs. At the back of the hill was a gate, its spiked top raised to permit entry. Lamps bled a golden light across the drive that led through it, wide enough to accommodate a horse-drawn cart or wide shipping carpet.

Miss Fetchkeep calmly walked through the gate. Ermin quickly followed. Rory halted just inside the gate, licking his lips. "This is far enough. And keep the gate open."

Miss Fetchkeep inclined her silvery head. "As you wish."

Emboldened, Ermin turned away from Rory. He wouldn't dare do anything to her in front of Miss Fetchkeep. "He's got Colin," she informed the headmistress.

"Not anymore. Would you like to see him?"

Ermin blinked in confusion. Rory's fingers seized her upper arm in a bruising grip. "You'll stay right here until the lady pays me."

"I think not." Miss Fetchkeep peeled off one of her gloves to reveal a metal arm underneath. Five metal fingers encircled Rory's wrist and squeezed. Rory cried out in shock and let go.

"You burned me!"

"Not intentionally," Miss Fetchkeep said as she let go.

Rory's eyes narrowed. "Nobody cheats Rory Smythe." He pulled a knife from his waistband and charged at Miss Fetchkeep.

"No!" Ermin cried out as Rory stabbed down with his blade.

Miss Fetchkeep stood there, smiling, as the knife sliced through her dress and hit the skin of her chest with a blunt clang. Rory dropped the knife. It clattered harmlessly to the ground, the blade's tip bent to one side.

"Wh-what?" he stammered. The gate clanged shut behind him. "Hey!"

Miss Fetchkeep's smile widened. "How clumsy of me! I must have knocked the lever by mistake."

"Miss Fetchkeep, are you hurt?" Ermin couldn't believe the headmistress was still standing, but she showed not the slightest sign of shock or distress. Not one spot of blood stained the fabric. She must be wearing armor beneath the gown, though why anyone would wear armor to a ball was beyond Ermin. *Unless she wasn't wearing any armor at all.*

"Come along, Mr. Smythe. You too, Ermin. I'll take the carpet, if you don't mind." Miss Fetchkeep held out a metal hand for the rope. "It belongs to the school, after all."

Ermin twisted the mooring rope in her hands. Standing up to the headmistress was nerve-racking, but she didn't want to let go of the carpet ever again. "Nobody wanted it. I fixed it."

"That's what I wanted to talk to you about—and why I asked Mr. Smythe to bring you here."

Ermin's mind reeled. Miss Fetchkeep had sent Rory to fetch her? Why bring her to Redemption Square and not the school? Miss Fetchkeep gently took the rope out of Ermin's hand and gestured her forward. "After you, my dear."

Miss Fetchkeep herded them into the side of the hill and up a wide stone ramp, her silver gown glowing phantom-like around her. Stone walls hemmed them in on either side. Rory stumbled along beside Ermin. From the way he clutched at his wrist, the burn must be bad.

"This is all your fault," Rory muttered out of the corner of his mouth. "Filthy wizard."

Fury exploded in Ermin. She knocked her fist against Rory's injured arm, making him gasp in pain. "Say that again."

Rory flashed his fangs in a weak leer. "Never thought you had it in you. Maybe I should have made you my lieutenant."

Ermin recoiled. She was nothing like Rory or his Rats. She tried to put as much distance as possible between them as they continued up the ramp.

A cavernous, rectangular room opened on their left, much larger than the draining platform above. It was an underground chamber dug into the side of the hill. A thick hose uncoiled from the room and ran up one side of the ramp like a giant black worm.

"That's the packing chamber," said Miss Fetchkeep.

That must be where they funneled the drained wizards' power into batteries to be sold as fuel. The ramp was big enough for a cart... or a tumbrel. The silvery glow from Miss Fetchkeep's gown illuminated the metal bars of a cage. The wings of her flying cape unfolded with a familiar hum. She collared Rory and rose into the air, dragging him over to the cage.

Rory struggled in her grasp. "What are you doing? Let me go!"

Miss Fetchkeep's steely hand propelled Rory into the cage. She pushed him inside and locked the door. Rory occupied one of the many cages stretched out in a row—cages for wizards. Colin wasn't inside any of them. Miss Fetchkeep must not have discovered his secret.

"It's clear that you are a menace and a threat," Miss Fetchkeep said to Rory. "You'll stay here until I decide what to do with you."

Rory would have been livid if he wasn't in so much pain.

He kicked at the bars, the silver toe of his boot clanging with each strike. "You owe me! You promised to pay me if I brought the girl to you!"

Miss Fetchkeep whirred over the cage. "Did I? I don't remember saying so. I don't do business with those I can't trust."

Ermin clenched her teeth to stop them from chattering as Miss Fetchkeep flew back toward her, thrumming like a giant insect. "Come along, dear. Colin is waiting."

Chapter Seventeen

"Where are you taking me, Miss Fetchkeep?" Ermin struggled to keep pace with the head-mistress as they hurried along the corridor.

"On a little trip to the future—your future."

What future was that, Ermin wondered. "I didn't pass the exams."

"I wonder if I've been thinking about your situation all wrong. All this fuss about magic and exams... it's all nonsense, once you think about it. Close your mouth, Ermin. It's not polite to gawk."

Never in her life had Ermin expected Miss Fetchkeep to say such things. It was as if the headmistress had wrapped her cold arm around Ermin's shoulders. Her cold metal arm.

A narrow ramp had taken them up a half level to a second chamber. Miss Fetchkeep ushered her inside. "In here."

This new chamber was smaller than the previous one. The stone walls had yielded to wrought iron bars and railings. Bluish light filtered through the room from a ring of storm lamps on iron brackets. An enormous metal box stood in the center of the chamber. Multicolored wires were bundled together in a thick cord that ran from the top of the box and branched out across the ceiling in a dizzying network. The thick black hose from the packing room was wedged into the bottom of the box. They must be directly behind the draining platform. This metal box must be the holding tank. Ermin felt sick just looking at it.

"As I was saying," Miss Fetchkeep continued, "the Guild does not consider students who struggle to master basic magi-technical skills as suitable candidates, but that's only a cover. In reality, the exams have less to do with aptitude and everything to do with control. There are only so many placements, so the Guild wants to decide who gets placed in what trade, and when. It's all about restricting the flow of applicants. That's why the qualifying exams exist. It's got nothing to do with talent or ability. Not a thing!"

It was one thing for a renegade bandit like Captain Cora-leone to criticize the Guild, it was quite another for the head-mistress of St. Anselm's to do so. If Miss Fetchkeep really felt this way, then why had she made Ermin take the exam three times?

"You're probably wondering why I went along with it. The fact is, I had no choice. The Guild maintains an iron grip on training and education. That's the way things were organized in the Old World, so that's the way they do it in Garrison Creek. They don't understand that we are not in Astoria. We could do things differently, modernize our operations, but those in power are stuck in their ways. Show them a new idea and they shut it down.

"That is why I set you up in business, Ermin. With your pronounced lack of magi-technical aptitude, you were never going to get the chance to study at the Guild or earn an apprenticeship. I decided to try something new, a little experiment, as it were. I gave you a workshop and sent you out to work on jobs, in hopes that you'd be able to master your trade on your own. I followed your development with interest. You did not disappoint. In fact, my little experiment quite exceeded my expectations."

Miss Fetchkeep's words struck a false note with Ermin. Why hadn't she let Ermin in on the secret if she'd truly wanted her to succeed? She could have supported Ermin instead of forcing Ermin to sneak around behind her back to try to secure a future for herself. It wasn't true that Miss Fetchkeep had set her up in business either. All she'd done was let her use the Old Chapel as her workshop. Ermin had built up her entire tool collection by herself. And because she had to keep her accounts secret, Ermin had lived in constant terror of being kicked out of school. Miss Fetchkeep hadn't made it easy for Ermin to succeed at this "little experiment." She'd made it easy for her to fail.

"What have you done to Colin, Miss Fetchkeep?"

Miss Fetchkeep let out a low croak of laughter. "Absolutely nothing! After all, I'm not the one with the transpositor, am I?"

Ermin's insides turned to ice. She'd never told Miss Fetchkeep what D'Arcy's machine was called. Miss Fetchkeep couldn't have known unless she'd seen it before. Far worse, she also seemed to know what it could do.

The two-noted call of a marsh cray pierced the air. In a flash, Ermin followed the sound to the other side of the holding tank, where she found Colin manacled to the power meter. He'd managed to loosen his gag enough to gasp out a few words.

"Miss Fetchkeep is in league with Rory! Don't trust her!"

A loud insect thrumming filled the air as Miss Fetchkeep settled down beside Colin. "Didn't anyone ever tell you that it's not nice to tattle?"

Ermin's fingers fumbled under her cape for the yellow dial as she aimed the transpositor at Miss Fetchkeep.

"It's no good trying to drain me. I'm not a wizard. And I think you'd find me rather impervious to zapping." Miss Fetchkeep let out a low laugh, as if she'd just told a joke.

"Let him go!" Ermin said through gritted teeth.

"Well, that depends entirely on you. I'm offering you a future far beyond your wildest imaginings. Yet you resist my every attempt to show it to you." Miss Fetchkeep flung a metal arm around Colin's neck. As she shifted her weight, a strange, metallic clang rang out.

Ermin recognized the sound instantly. "You're the one who tried to stop us in D'Arcy's office that night."

"*Mr.* D'Arcy," Miss Fetchkeep corrected her. "He recognized Colin in doll shape, of course, but I told him that I would take care of the situation myself. Unfortunately, I found out too late that you'd fixed the unrequisitioned flying carpet he'd stashed in his office."

Panic whittled down Ermin's thoughts into three sharp points.

One: Miss Fetchkeep was not who she said she was. Far from being a supporter, Miss Fetchkeep was working with D'Arcy, the Wharf Rats, and possibly the Magistrates.

Two: Miss Fetchkeep hadn't yet confiscated the transpositor. Why not?

Three: Georgie knew where Ermin was, but Miss Fetchkeep didn't know this.

Ermin didn't yet know how these three things all added up or how they could be worked to her advantage. She needed to learn more. She arranged her expression into the careful blankness she'd used so often when readying herself for a scolding. She'd never noticed how oddly doll-like Miss Fetchkeep's eyes were, like two black buttons pressed onto an unyielding face.

"What do you want?"

"Much the same thing as you: a future I can control. It's a great pity that Mr. D'Arcy let himself be goaded into revealing so much of our plan prematurely. He became addicted and untrustworthy."

Miss Fetchkeep had as good as admitted that she knew what D'Arcy was doing with the transpositor. She'd also sat in when D'Arcy had tested Colin with that costly new bewitcher. Of course D'Arcy had used a special bewitcher to test students. It was probably another bit of Magistrate gear, calibrated to trap wizards. How many other orphan wizards had been tested in this way? Miss Fetchkeep had an excellent record for placing students. What if the wizarding students hadn't been placed at all, but had been drained of their power after being tested by D'Arcy? The small skeleton lying under the bushes in the Scrawlings flashed across her mind.

"You knew that D'Arcy was draining wizards and did nothing to stop him."

Miss Fetchkeep dipped her head in acknowledgment. "Brava, Ermin, but you haven't guessed everything. Not yet."

Miss Fetchkeep lifted off her shining silver mask. Then she raised two fingers to her hairline and pulled off her face. Underneath was a square metal frame embedded into living flesh, enclosing a pair of steam-powered eyeballs and a hissing, gear-laden mouth.

Colin stiffened, his eyes going wide with shock. Ermin felt certain he would have screamed if Miss Fetchkeep's hand wasn't clamped tight over his mouth.

"Don't look so shocked, dear girl! There's nothing to be frightened of. I would have thought that you'd be pleased to find yourself in the company of a mechanical person. Here—I have something for you."

She pulled out a necklace, the same necklace Ermin had

given to Colin for safekeeping before entering Frank's Hotel. The same necklace that Denny had kept in his pocket before returning it to her. He'd still been carrying it when Miss Fetchkeep accosted him at the fair to ask about her.

"You've been using that necklace to track us."

Miss Fetchkeep's mouth-gears clicked upward in a hideous non-smile. "I was just trying to protect my investment. It's a good thing I found you when I did, or you'd be trapped working for Denny forever. You've always wanted to become a mechanic. Well, now you are one. Starting today, you'll work for me. For your first assignment, you're going to transfer all the power in that holding tank to me using the transpositor."

An icy finger of dread trailed down Ermin's back. "What? Why?"

"Isn't it obvious?" Miss Fetchkeep's mouth-gears clicked while she talked. "With that kind of power, I can unseat the Magistrates and the Guild and transform this settlement into a paragon of efficiency and prosperity, one that Queen Georgina will no longer be able to ignore. I will be sure to drive that lesson home to her when I sail back as an ambassador to the Astorian court. Of course, I'll need a good mechanic by my side —one that I can trust. Didn't I tell you that you'd always have a home with me?"

Miss Fetchkeep's terrible scheme unfolded before Ermin like a battle map. Miss Fetchkeep's strategy was brilliant... and terrible. Unlike human wizards, a cyborg wizard would never dry up or suffer from blowback. A cyborg wizard could easily regenerate all the power it needed from its own internal electrical circuits. No one would be able to stop it, not the Magistrates or the Resistance. Miss Fetchkeep would surely eliminate both of them before she sailed for Astoria so they couldn't take over the settlement during her absence. Poor Queen Georgina would never realize the truth about her new ambassador until it was too late.

Miss Fetchkeep's doll-button eyes bored into Ermin's. "Do not think that you can refuse me. I can wring Colin's neck as easily as a chicken's. His wizardry, powerful as it is, cannot save him from death."

"You'll never get away with it. The Magistrates will stop you."

"I think not. They're far too busy hunting down the Resistance. Once I've transformed, it will be too late. I'll be far too powerful to stop."

Ermin regarded the Fetchkeep cyborg with a steely loathing. Everything she'd ever told Ermin was a lie. Instead of being concerned about Ermin's or the other orphans' futures, all she'd been thinking about was her own. Georgie had been right about her all along. Miss Fetchkeep had encouraged Ermin just enough to keep her hoping while undermining her self-confidence by forcing her to take tests she'd never pass, or slipping derogatory comments in between snippets of praise. She'd gotten rid of Georgie, the one student who'd been brave enough to stand up to her, thereby eliminating a potential threat. The only reason she'd given Ermin the workshop was to groom her. She'd groomed D'Arcy in exactly the same way, encouraging him to experiment upon himself even as he became more and more addicted to the power. Miss Fetchkeep didn't care, so long as he proved that a wizard's power could be transferred to others. Then all she needed was an inventive mechanic to bring her master plan to fruition.

Ermin couldn't let Miss Fetchkeep take over the settlement, but she couldn't let her kill Colin either. Miss Fetchkeep didn't know there was still a partially full orbulet inside the transpositor. Ermin couldn't use it against the cyborg, but she could give it to Colin.

She forced herself to look defeated. "All right."

"No!" Colin cried out. Ermin locked eyes with him, silently willing him to trust her.

"That's right!" Miss Fetchkeep clapped her metal hands together. "I knew you'd see the value of my offer."

Ermin unstrapped her blanket roll. Miss Fetchkeep seized her arm in a freezing grip. "What are you doing?"

"I need my tools to do my work." This explanation seemed to mollify Miss Fetchkeep, and she let Ermin go. *Good.* The longer she believed she had won Ermin over, the better. "And you'll have to unshackle him." Ermin jerked her head at Colin, hoping that the cyborg couldn't hear the loud beating of her heart.

"I think not. You're going to drain him too."

Ermin felt like she was about to be sick. She swallowed hard and forced a false calm into her voice. "The iron manacles will act as a damper, preventing me from transferring the power to you."

The cyborg thought about this. "I'll unshackle him from the storage cell, but the manacles stay on."

Ermin shook her head. "I can't drain him, not while he's wearing iron."

She shot Colin a meaningful glare. *Get ready.* Whether he understood her or not was hard to tell, as he made no reply.

"After I unshackle him, you'll start the transfer immediately."

Ermin gave a reluctant nod, though inwardly she was cheering. Once the manacles were off, she could juice up Colin with whatever power remained in the orange vial. She didn't think that the cyborg would harm her. She—*it*—didn't know how to use the transpositor. That's why it hadn't confiscated it. It needed Ermin to operate it. As soon as she and Colin attacked, the cyborg would go for Colin since it needed Ermin to operate the transpositor. Only it would find itself up against a very angry, juiced-up wizard.

Rain hammered against the draining platform. An atmospheric river, from the sounds of it. A few drops hit Ermin's face. She looked up. There was a hole in the ceiling. A goose's head poked through, her beak bathed in a purple glow. Georgie!

The cyborg bent to unlock Colin's manacles. While it was fiddling with the keys, Ermin flashed Georgie the thumbs-up before exaggeratedly pointing the notched end of the transpositor, fill side up, at Colin. Georgie's long neck writhed up and down in a show of enthusiasm.

The cyborg straightened, its hands clamped on Colin's shoulders. "Hook us up. Don't think that you can fool me. I know very well that D'Arcy connected himself to the machine by means of a wire."

"That's not how the machine works anymore. I modified it."

Miss Fetchkeep hesitated. Ermin pressed on. "I have to drain Colin first before I can transfer the power to you. It doesn't happen simultaneously anymore."

"I'll just keep hold of him until you do."

Ermin thought wildly. "Do you have any iron parts?"

Slowly, the cyborg withdrew.

Ermin's heart was pounding so fast, she was afraid she might black out. She took a few deep, steadying breaths. "Don't be afraid," she told Colin. "This will be exactly like that time at John Smith's forge."

Colin's eyes widened in sudden understanding. "Ah, well. It's been good knowing you."

Ermin's trigger hand shook. This might be their final goodbye. It probably would be, once Georgie told him about Ermin's plans for the transpositor. "You too."

She fired. An orange jet streaked toward Colin. The cyborg

let out a startled cry, but blasts of purple fire from Georgie's beak distracted it. It rose into the air with a menacing hum. With a terrible cry, Colin launched himself at the cyborg, glowing as red as a burning phoenix. The missile Colin had become would have eliminated even the most powerful magi-technician or wizard, but the cyborg remained intact as he struck. Only its steam leg bore any signs of damage, a small crack that rained sparks. Colin steamed upward and blasted straight through the ceiling. Rain gushed down, drenching Ermin and the cyborg both.

Ermin twisted the yellow dial to stop herself from being electrocuted and tucked the transpositor into her cloak. She hopped onto the carpet and was airborne in seconds. She flew around the room as the Fetchkeep cyborg hovered in the air, tilting to one side. One of its cape's wings had been bent when Colin had hit it, so that it had difficulty flying straight.

Georgie plunked herself down on the carpet beside Ermin and shifted into human shape. "You've got to let me destroy that machine before the cyborg gets hold of it."

Ermin swerved around one of Miss Fetchkeep's lopsided lunges. Colin rained red sparks down on the cyborg and it withdrew, its damaged leg sparking more wildly than ever. "It can be used for good. I know it can."

"Give the transpositor to me, now!" Georgie commanded.

There was a boom from the center of the room. Colin's bombardments had set the holding tank on fire. Thick smoke poured through the hole in the ceiling like a beacon. It wouldn't be long before it was spotted by the Magistrates.

"Georgie, take Colin and go. The Magistrates will be here any minute."

Georgie shifted back to goose form, and with a honk of despair flung herself into the air. A round of argumentative cackling and a peck finally convinced Colin to stop firing on

Miss Fetchkeep. Ermin watched with a rush of emotions as they flew away. Georgie had chosen to save herself and Colin. The break was complete.

The cyborg trained its black, expressionless eyes on Ermin. Sparks ran down its metal leg like blood. "You will pay for what you have done."

Ermin's deception had unleashed the cyborg's fury, but it couldn't afford to kill Ermin, not yet. Not until the power from dozens of wizards flowed through its circuits. But if the transpositor no longer existed, it would no longer present a danger to wizards, to the Creek, or to Queen Georgina. As much as Ermin fought against it, destroying the transpositor was the only way to defeat the cyborg.

With a scream, Ermin jumped, the upward motion tugging at her steer straps. The carpet shot through the hole that Colin had made. She banked and came around just as the cyborg emerged from the hole. The rain pounded like nails against its metal skin. Ermin pushed wet strands of hair from her face. This was it. She had the cyborg exactly where she wanted it. She unstrapped the transpositor, keeping it protected under her cape while she switched on the yellow dial. She had to make sure the cyborg was good and wet for what she had in mind.

The cyborg hovered before her, mouth-gears working furiously.

"Work with me, Ermin, and I promise you will have a place at the Guild, with the best mechanics." The cyborg shifted gears, its voice growing smooth as it tried to convince Ermin to listen. "They'll fight over a mind like yours, a mind that can reverse magical circuits to create a new weapon. That sort of mind is invaluable. Beyond price."

The cyborg spoke with Miss Fetchkeep's voice, but there was no Miss Fetchkeep. There never had been. Like an evil conductor, the cyborg-pretending-to-be-Miss-Fetchkeep had orchestrated acts of chaos and ruin in its quest for power. It had lied about Ermin's abilities in order to make her stay at St. Anselm's. Now it hoped to use false praise to weaken her into compliance. As soon as the cyborg got what it wanted, it would turn on her the way it had turned on everyone else.

But Ermin no longer needed a monster's praise or promises. She was stronger than the cyborg knew. She was strong enough to resist. Strong enough to steal back her own life.

Damp cold rose around her like a phantom's breath. She had one chance to get this right. For her friends, for the wizards and orphans of the Creek, for Queen Georgina. For herself.

"How does it feel to know that your conquest will fail, all because of me—the remedial pupil who could never pass? Because *I* will fail, Miss Fetchkeep. I'll fail you just as surely as you have failed me."

The cyborg shrieked like a bird of prey. It darted forward, its fingers raking the air. Its steam leg sparked and fizzed as rainwater rolled down it, making it the perfect conductor.

Ermin threw the transpositor with all her might. It shattered against the cyborg's leg and exploded. A crackling, jagged net of electricity enveloped the creature's body. The cyborg was strong. It fought the current. It bucked and kicked in desperate fury, but the crackling net held fast, burning the flying cape away to cinders. Clutching at empty air, the cyborg fell, trailing black smoke behind it like a comet just as a convoy of black-robed Magistrates landed in Redemption Square.

Chapter Eighteen

Ermin descended the pink stone steps of the meeting house, fingering the Magistrates' Scholar Medallion that hung around her neck. Greetings and congratulations rang out around her but she could hardly take them in. All she wanted was to do was to get away. Being the focus of so much attention was dangerous. Every orphan in the Creek knew that. She broke into a run and started for Old Town, hoping to lose herself in the familiar, winding maze of alleyways and lanes. She didn't have to worry about Wharf Rats anymore. Snarl had made sure of that. With Rory in prison, she'd been crowned the new Rat Queen and Ermin was under her protection. No Rat would dare to tangle with her.

No matter how fast she ran, Dr. Dean's words still rang in her ears.

"You have helped to rid Garrison Creek of a terrible menace. If you had not outwitted the wizard-cyborg with your inventive and ingenious use of mechanics, we would now be facing a hostile takeover of our settlement."

Dr. Dean had assumed the cyborg was a wizard because of

the huge amount of wizard's residue the Magistrates had discovered inside the draining platform. The rain had stopped their tracking fog from going beyond the hole in the ceiling, so Colin and Georgie were safe. Only Ermin had taken note of the two geese waddling across Redemption Square in full view of the Magistrates, gobbling up stray crusts as they went. A lone human finger had trailed from the smaller goose's wing.

"Today, we admit you into the small, select circle of Magistrates' scholars as a token of our gratitude," Dr. Dean had said as he hung the medallion around her neck. "An award that funds four years of study at the Guild's Apprenticeship Academy in a trade of your choice. We don't need to guess which one you will pick!" A wave of polite laughter rippled through the meeting house.

Four years of fully funded study at the Academy was more than Ermin had ever dreamed of. Her friends had cheered and clapped the hardest of all: Snarl, the new Queen of the Rats, with Mouse and Denny at her side. Only Colin and Georgie had been missing.

Ermin could guess how winning a Magistrate-funded scholarship might look to them. Still, it hurt to think that after all they'd been through, they couldn't even bring themselves to talk to her. They'd been avoiding her ever since the battle. Denny and Snarl had told her not to worry, that they'd come around, but Ermin was not so sure. Maybe they believed that she'd sold them out to the Magistrates. That thought hurt more than their silence.

It was amazing how quickly she moved through the streets now that she didn't have to attach herself to unsuspecting marks. She slowed to a walk as the cramped and crooked network of lanes closed in around her. She picked the strongest-looking drainpipe she could find and shimmied up. A blast of rain hit her face, cooling after the stuffy ceremonial hall. A network of streets radiated out in a web, with houses and people caught in its damp strands. She'd never wanted to fly as badly as she did right now, but she'd left the carpet behind at Denny's. She couldn't very well have worn it during the ceremony. She crouched down between two chimney pots for shelter, searching her pockets for a handkerchief to wipe her glasses. Her fingers curled around a scrap of paper. She pulled it out. It was the response to their ad that Denny had cut out from the *Sentinel*, the message they'd never been able to decipher. Georgie had wanted to throw it out, but Ermin had kept it.

Baker's dozen wanted for party. Balanced scales only.

Why did the phrase *baker's dozen* pull at her so?

She cast her mind back to when she'd last heard it. It had been at the mill, when the Widow Pettigrew had wheeled into the shop to place an order for thirteen bags of flour. What occasion could possibly require the purchase of so much flour? The Magistrates' Ball, maybe. Surely the Widow Pettigrew hadn't volunteered to be the baker, not if she was a guest. Come to think of it, Ermin hadn't seen the Widow at the ball. She would have been instantly recognizable because of Pickle.

The ad mentioned a baker's dozen, and the party had been held on December 13. Was that a coincidence? And what did *balanced scales* mean?

Her thoughts circled back to the night when Denny had tried to teach her about the constellations. He'd talked about Libra weighing out justice with her scales. Here in the Creek, the Resistance fought with the Magistrates to rebalance the scales of justice.

Thirteen. Balanced scales. Justice.

Ermin's mind raced with excitement. Georgie had said that

the newspaper ad was written in code. What if it told of a Resistance attack at the Magistrates' Ball on December 13?

She thought back to the explosions at Frank's Hotel. A much bigger incendiary device than her smoke bombs had caused it... or maybe a lot of smaller, strategically planted bombs. What if the Widow Pettigrew hadn't been buying flour but transporting gunpowder in preparation for the attack?

Where could the gunpowder have come from? It couldn't be manufactured at the mill. It would be too risky to buy it from a merchant, since merchants were required to keep strict records of any arms purchases. They must have found a different supplier. Who in the settlement would dare to take such a risk?

Maybe the supplier didn't live in the settlement at all.

In the Scrawlings, Captain Coraleone had told her that what her gang really needed was people who could fix things: "Most of the people I live among are blasted fools when it comes to fixing."

Blasted wizarding fools, more like! Gray powder trickling from a keg, the assembly line with its funnels and sacks, the forest fire that had been snuffed out so quickly, the campsite that had never been invaded by bandits—because who made up the majority of bandits? Wizards who'd been dumped in the Scrawlings. Captain Coraleone hadn't taken the canoe on a test ride. She'd been making a delivery to the Resistance, carrying a cargo of gunpowder-filled sacks.

But where? Ermin paced back and forth across the roof. It would be too risky to make the drop-off directly at the mill, even with Sclaw to act as guardian. Someone would be sure to notice all the late-night comings and goings. No, the drop-off point was more likely to be located in a neighborhood where shady dealings were commonplace, where threats held currency and money could buy you protection.

She stopped mid-pace. Her fingers rummaged around in her pockets for the new lock picks Snarl had given her. They were there, along with the wood raveler, a rare tool that could double as a weapon. The Rat Queen's protection was limited to Wharf Rat territory. Ermin would need a weapon where she was going.

Pennyluck Place never slept. Most of the Faeling businesses operated after sundown, so the streets were thick with traffic. Light spilled from the surrounding shops, makeshift cellar taverns, and gaming dens. A whiff of dream-smoke wafted out from behind the brightly curtained doorway of a smoking den. Ermin held her breath as she hurried past, nearly knocking into a group of Faeling children playing a raucous game of blindfold buff. A group of artists in colorful masks walked by, their arms full of painted canvases. A Faeling glim walker guided their steps, light beaming from her third eye.

Ermin recognized the little cottage belonging to Sclaw's mother at once. Glowbushes still grew in the window boxes. The warmth radiating from their leaves steamed the windows. Any resident would have taken regular cuttings to warm the cottage, or else some enterprising thief would have cut them down. Their overgrown state confirmed Ermin's suspicions that no one was living here and the cottage was under protection. Best not to enter from the street.

There was just enough room between the cottage and the next building for her to squeeze between them. She entered a small yard that housed a private washhouse and privy—a luxury in these parts, where it was common for dozens of families to share. Ermin opened the privy door. The air inside was musty, with none of the stink she'd have expected from frequent use. The washhouse had a sloping floor that led to a drain, and housed a sink and a metal bath. She shone a glim light over the enamel surfaces. No grime. Outside, grass and weeds had grown up around the cesspool. It would make a perfect landing place for a flying canoe.

She waited and watched for a few more minutes, listening for footfalls or the scrape and click of talons. Freezing rain dripped off the end of her nose. When enough time had passed to satisfy her that she hadn't been followed, she withdrew her lock picks from her pocket and went to work on the back door.

Inside the cottage, the same musty smell greeted her. Her breath smoked in the unheated air. The single room was completely bare except for piles of sacks. Thick white curtains were drawn across the windows. Boot prints and three-taloned footprints left geometrical patterns in the thick coating of dust on the floor. Ermin's own boot prints would hardly be noticed. She selected one of the sacks and carried it out to the privy, where she slashed it open with the pointed end of a lock pick. A quick flash from her glim box showed a seam of gray powder. So it was Sclaw who ferried sacks of gunpowder from the cottage to the mill. There was only one piece of the puzzle left to slot into place. The powder cost money, and the gang who protected the cottage would have to be paid off. Where did the money come from?

The Orphan Fund!

She'd been there when the Widow Pettigrew had dropped off her monthly "donation" at the mill. She wondered how many of the mill's other customers did the same, carrying away bags of "flour" for the Resistance? There might be a far more extensive network of wizards and their supporters than anyone had ever realized. She thought of Essey, running from her the night of the ball. She hadn't been working for Mrs. Brack; she was an undercover operative. She'd left the great hall to set off bombs. The mill wasn't some outpost of renegade activity; it was the beating heart of the Resistance.

Ermin tipped most of the gunpowder down the privy, leaving just enough to prove her claims. Outside, the sky was noticeably lighter. The millers would soon be rising. Ermin suppressed a shiver. Facing the millers was one thing, but having Sclaw discover that she'd broken into her mother's cottage didn't bear thinking about.

Ermin heard the Don River long before she reached the end of Picking Cork Lane. It sounded louder, filling the air with a constant roar. The river watchers would have to open the sluice gates if the water got any higher. The gears of the mill wheel thudded and creaked. Coils of woodsmoke rose from the kitchen chimney, where Sclaw and Essey were no doubt preparing breakfast for the millers and—if Ermin's guess was right—at least two other guests. Make that three, she corrected herself, as the Widow Pettigrew's battered top hat appeared at the window.

Ermin hugged the half-empty sack of gunpowder. She was about to spill what she knew about the entire smuggling operation. There was no telling how the wizards would react. They'd be focused on the Resistance, on keeping it safe and plugging the breach, as it were. Not even the Magistrates' Medallion would be enough to save her if they decided to strike.

Maybe she should just walk away. Only this was her best chance—maybe her only chance—to try to convince Georgie and Colin that she was still on their side. All she needed to do was to explain what she knew and reassure them that she'd never betray them. The bag of gunpowder was proof of her word.

She squared her shoulders and crossed the road. She forced her legs up the steps, one at a time, all the way up to the front door. The bell jingled as she entered the shop. It was empty, as she'd expected, until Sclaw appeared, her unsheathed talons scraping the floor.

"We're not open yet. Come back in an hour."

Ermin craned her neck to try to see into the kitchen beyond. Sclaw's wings rose in a protective arc to block the view but not before Ermin caught a glimpse of Essey, Soon-Yi, Hetty, the Widow Pettigrew, Georgie, and Colin all seated together round the kitchen table.

Ermin ducked under Sclaw's restraining wing and ran into the kitchen. "I'm not your enemy and I've come to prove it. Here's my pledge."

She tossed the sack onto the table. Gunpowder billowed out, covering toast, porridge, and marmalade in an ashen blanket. Sclaw's growl and the stiff silence around the table told Ermin that she was unwelcome. Only Pickle barked out a greeting.

"I know that you coordinated the bombing of Frank's Hotel on December thirteenth. I know about your secret smuggling operation with Captain Coraleone, and the private Orphan donations to fund it. I know that nobody lives at the cottage in Pennyluck Place. The Resistance uses it as a warehouse to stockpile arms. I know that Sclaw ferries bags of gunpowder from the cottage to the mill, and that the Widow Pettigrew uses her chair to make deliveries to various Resistance cells. If I was going to betray you, don't you think I would have told the Magistrates all I know instead of coming to you?"

A deathly silence fell over the room.

"What do you want?" Soon-Yi asked.

"To help!" Ermin's voice cracked. "What do you think?"

Soon-Yi gestured angrily at the medallion that swung free

of Ermin's collar. "You made your choice as soon as you let them hang that thing around your neck. You can't play on two sides at once."

"Why not? Isn't that what you're all doing, pretending to be one thing while you're really something else?"

"The chittling has a point," said Sclaw. "One way or another, we're all playing make-believe. Besides, the Magistrates would have been here by now if she'd told."

"Give back your little medal to the Magistrates, and then we'll talk," said Soon-Yi.

Ermin straightened. "No, I won't give up my scholarship. Why should I? It's not as if you or the other wizards can teach me anything." Sclaw let out a rusty bark of laughter. She quickly turned it into a cough at a glare from Soon-Yi. "You can trust me. I've already proved my good faith by keeping my friends' secrets."

Colin lifted his head and looked straight at her.

Ermin's chest heaved up and down as she confronted her two friends. "Don't you dare shut me out, not after everything we've been through. How could you believe that I'd ever tell on you?"

Georgie let out a short laugh. "Well, let me think. Perhaps it's because you've joined the Magistrates?"

"I didn't know that they were going to award me with a Guild scholarship, but I'm not about to throw it away, now that I have it. I've never worked for the Magistrates and I never will."

The Widow Pettigrew's eyes drilled into Ermin's. "Why do you want to help?"

"Because I hate the Magistrates! They just want to control all the magic for themselves. That's why they lie about wizards being dangerous. The Magistrates are the real danger—to wizards and everyone else."

"I, for one, am curious," said Hetty. "How did you find us?"

Ermin told them how Georgie had placed a classified ad in the *Sentinel*, hoping to get in touch with the Resistance, but hadn't been able to decipher the coded reply. She detailed the various clues that had helped her solve the puzzle, leading her first to the cottage and then to the mill. She said nothing about the transpositor, the way she'd clung to it, convinced that it could be used for good. Neither did Georgie. That had to mean something.

"Wait here," Soon-Yi said when she'd finished. She disappeared into a back room and returned carrying a purse. She thrust it out at Ermin. "This should buy your loyalty... and your silence."

Ermin backed away. "I didn't come here to be paid off."

"All the same, you'll take it. I've got it marked as a reward for unspecified services in our ledgers. If you inform on us and we're captured, you'll be implicated as an accomplice."

Face burning, Ermin slid the purse into her pocket. Soon-Yi was treating her like a blackmailer. She turned to Colin and Georgie. "You know I'd never inform on you. You have to believe me."

"Believe you?" Georgie scoffed. "You belong to the Magistrates now. Why should we believe anything you say?"

"Because I've done nothing wrong. You bagged your future by joining the Resistance. Don't I deserve the same chance?"

"You'd already bagged a perfectly good chance with Denny. You could work out of the forge forever. You don't need a Guild scholarship from the Magistrates. What if they force you to take a loyalty pledge? Whose side will you be on?"

"I'll leave if they ask me to take a pledge."

"If you refuse to take it, they'll lock you up. Leave now."

"How many times do I have to tell you, you don't have to worry about me?"

"So you say." Georgie folded her arms across her chest.

Colin bit his lip.

"You'd best get back to your school." Soon-Yi's lips curled as she spoke the word *school*. It was as if she'd drawn a line down the middle of the room and Ermin stood on the wrong side of it.

Sclaw let out a disapproving harrumph. "You may be my sister, Soon-Yi, but you're wrong to deny this girl. Who knows? It may be useful to have a plant inside the Academy."

"Keep out of it, Sclaw!" warned Soon-Yi.

"Fine, fine!" Sclaw held up her wings in surrender.

Ermin faced Soon-Yi. "You're wrong about me. I've never spilled on my wizard friends, and I never will, no matter what you think. Don't forget that we defeated the cyborg with no help from you or your precious Resistance."

"Enough!"

Ermin pointed at Soon-Yi. "And I'd make a terrific spy."

Colin caught her eye. He was smiling and nodding. That small gesture was all the encouragement Ermin needed.

"You can always send word to me at Denny's. I'll be helping out at the forge in my spare time." Holding her head high, she walked from the room. She'd nearly made it to the door when she heard the scrape of Sclaw's talons behind her. She turned to face her, startled by the gentle smile that creased Sclaw's face.

"I don't believe you're a traitor."

"Try telling that to them!"

Sclaw let out a chuckle. "That medallion of yours has given them a bit of a shock. It might take a while before they come around, but don't waste your time trying to convince them that you're right. It's enough to know it within yourself." Sclaw's wings gave Ermin's shoulders a gentle squeeze before guiding her out the door.

Ermin stumbled down the stairs, unsure of what had just happened. The Don River crested and foamed like a charge of stallions riding to battle. The roar of the water boomed deep inside her chest so that she felt like an instrument of its fury. The towpath was clear of traffic. No barges would be hauled today, not after the attacks on Frank's Hotel and Redemption Square. If only she could be sure of Colin and Georgie! What if Sclaw was wrong and they refused to ever talk to her again?

Georgie hadn't ratted her out, though, and Colin had smiled at her. Though bruised and tenuous, their connection still held; she was sure of it. If it did, then neither the Magistrates nor the Resistance could break it.

Ermin left the towpath. Quiet replaced the water's rushing boom. She could see her way through—to the next step, at least. As a Guild student, she would have no need for bargains and accounts. She'd be able to practice her craft out in the open, a shadow apprentice no longer. She stretched out her hands: a mechanic's hands, a fighter's hands, a student's hands, eager to take hold of the world and crack it open to see how everything worked. She couldn't wait for school to start.

Acknowledgments

Like many writers, I owe a huge debt of gratitude to the many people who encouraged and supported me during the writing of this book. Some of them encouraged me before I even knew I was a writer.

For my elementary school principal, Laura Schissler, who 'published' my Wizard of Oz fanfics in Grade 2, and made me promise to never throw them out. (I still have them.)

For my mother, Sheila Browne, who gave me my first library card at age 5; for my father, Doug Browne, for sharing his love of history and Toronto with me; and my brother, Tim Browne, for all the business talks in Muskoka over Christmas.

Many thanks to my editors, Dawn Loewen and Jen McIntyre, and my book cover designer, Jessica Bell. Their brilliant and insightful work made this book better at every turn, and their patience with a newbie author was greatly appreciated.

For my best friend, Kate McQuiggan, who cheerfully volunteered for beta reading duty, and was always ready to engage in wild storyboarding sessions to fix a plot hole or build a better character. This book never would have made it this far without her eagle-eyed feedback and lion-hearted support.

Many thanks to Dr. Gillian Turnbull, Director of Writing and Publishing at the University of King's College, for an invaluable manuscript critique, and many discussions about the publishing industry, women writers, and writing craft.

Many thanks to the Barker and Vise families for the generous loan of their farm, where the bulk of this book was revised, and many excellent meals were shared, and my clients, Ann Black, Bob Brandeis and Nancy and Jonathan Barker (again), who put up with far too many rescheduled appointments.

Thanks also to The Creative Academy for Writers for their warm and welcoming writing community, and to ALLi: The Alliance of Independent Authors, who taught me how to self-publish books, and run an author business.

And last but not least, I give daily thanks for my partner of 14 wonderful years, Allison Cameron, for always encouraging me to get my work out there. Look, I finally listened!

About the Author

Linda Browne is an LGBTQ+ author of (mostly) middle grade and young adult science fiction fantasy. Her work has been longlisted in The Times/Chicken House Children's Fiction Competition, and she's also been a finalist in CANSCAIP's Writing for Children Competition. Her debut MG steampunk novel, *Shadow Apprentice*, was a finalist in the 2024 Wishing Shelf Book Awards. Linda lives in Toronto with her partner, and far too many books and plants.

Find out more at her website: www.lindabrowne.ca, where you can also **sign up for her monthly newsletter and get a free eBook**.

~

Enjoyed the book?

Please consider leaving a short review where you like to buy or talk about books. This will help more readers discover Linda's books.

You can also request Linda's books from your local library or order them from your local bookstore. Every gesture of support counts, and is greatly appreciated!